Three

Against

The

Darkness

Leon Michaels

Books by Leon Michaels

The Path Home

From the Mists of Darkness

Task Force Nemesis

Tales From The Bench

The Hanover Throne

The Echelon Factor

The Morbius Expedition

The Bellus Project

"The Crane Equation Trilogy"

The Crane Equation: The Early Years

The Crane Equation: Rebuilding a Nation

The Crane Equation: The Crane Legacy

"The Black Ops Series"

Operation Damocles

Operation Dokkaebi

Operation Yofune-Nushi

Operation Kartikeya

The Black Orchid

"The Twenty-First Special Operations Group"

Book One: Family

Book Two: Operators

Author's Comments

Humanity is and always shall be a victim of their time. Each generation, each era brings with it a different set of morals and values which at times can almost seem draconian considering the world at whole.

What I have tried to depict with this tale is in some quarters perverse in nature but in others without fault. It all depends on where the reader is standing at the time. It also depends on the context of the story which I hope I have expressed well enough for the reader to understand this story does not take place in any manner considered normal.

One hundred or even seventy-five years ago much of what the reader might find as perverse today was considered normal by the standards of that time. It takes an understanding of history as it really was to consider that what once was could be once again.

It also takes a basic understanding of human nature to understand that evil lurks behind the mask of righteousness if the rules of civilization are tossed out the window. Many would say I'm wrong and some would call me a heathen for even considering such things, but to say there is not a spark of possibility in my statement is the height of arrogance, if not ignorance.

Mankind is a parasite, a blight upon this blue planet orbiting the sun. We rip, tear and otherwise destroy the world on which we live without giving anything back in return. Yet the only thing we can possibly give back is ourselves as our bodies return to the soil to nurture it. We give so little in return for so much.

The hero of this tale is caught between civilization and barbarism. His desires and morals. And at a time when the victim was willing, his morals battled his desires as civilization around him crumbled into barbarism.

I can only hope I told the tale in a proper manner.

Leon Michaels

Acknowledgements

As always to my bride for tolerating my long
hours
In my small office banging away on my
computer
Keyboard even if only I read what I write.

To Mike O...... Who pointed out obvious
Errors in editing and asked for more which
Led to over 500 more words.

This is a work of Fiction. Any similarities to individuals' past or present is unintentional and purely a coincidence. Any similarities to any individual in the future is pure Karma.

This page left blank on purpose!

But if I wrote that,

The page isn't blank!

Wednesday, April 12th

It's the End of the World as we know it.

Wednesday, the twelfth of April started like any other day, but it would end in turmoil. Eight cargo/container ships, three off the East coast, three off the West coast and two in the Gulf of Mexico reached their positions outside United States waters and each vessel launched two modified SCUD missiles armed with nuclear warheads towards specific points above the country. Each detonated within seconds of each other high in the atmosphere creating an umbrella of Electro-Magnetic Pulse effectively shutting down the country. They detonated at 10:03 Central Daylight Savings Time catching the majority of U.S. workers at work, away from their homes.

Civilian aircraft without hardened electronics fell from the sky killing thousands of people on the planes and on the ground. In the Los Angeles Basin, the second wave of rush hour traffic was brought to a flaming stand still as engines had their electronic ignition systems shut down which not only shut down the power steering systems but also killed the electronic anti-lock braking systems making it nearly impossible to stop a vehicle from colliding with another. Semi-tractor-trailer rigs rolled over the top of smaller vehicles due to their inability to stop because of the inertia of their heavy loads. Fuel tanks ruptured and sparking metal on concrete created an inferno that leaped from car to car consuming anyone who were unable to escape their vehicular coffins.

Law enforcement personal could only stand helplessly by as they had no manner of mobility except by foot and no communications except for face to face. Emergency services were in the same situation as fire trucks and ambulances were frozen in their parking spaces. In hospitals across the country, patients on life support died because even the back-up generators for the hospitals had been affected by the EM Pulse. Some would say that those who died within the first hour after the attack were the lucky ones.

Parents across the nation were in panic as their children were in school often miles away. It was never known if all the children were reunited with their parents, but some husbands and wives never made it home during the chaos that followed. The first twenty-four to forty-eight hours were considered the calmest or safest of the time after the event as people waited for the government to fix the problems and return life back to them as before. But that was not going to happen.

History would record this day simply as "The Event". Others took the title to an R.E.M. song to describe that day: "It's the End of the World as We know it."

April 13 to April 18

Stay or leave?

It had rained the night before the event, and Kevin Barnes knew it would be a waste of time and fuel in his truck to only come back home to his apartment due to the mud, and other problems associated with doing construction at this particular worksite. He was home when the event occurred.

Kevin Barnes did not consider himself anyone special. He was twenty-three years of age, single without a girlfriend at this time, and worked as a carpenter as his day job, and once a month as an Infantry Sergeant in the National Guard. He had joined the Guard at age eighteen and was in Afghanistan by age twenty. He didn't see much action in Afghanistan since his unit was mostly doing base security work and he came home finding the economy was heading into the crapper. Kevin was able to keep his head above water by doing a lot of handyman type work around town when construction jobs like the one he was home from were not available.

The Standard Operating Procedure for Kevin's Guard unit was to report for duty as soon as possible in case of such event except Kevin lived thirty-three miles from his unit's armory. He laid all his gear out in his apartment's living room in case his unit's vehicles were operational and they came for him. As he waited, he began to lay out the items he had stashed for a rainy day. Since returning from Afghanistan he had purchased a semi-automatic version of the AK-47 and had over five hundred rounds of ammunition for it plus a SigArms P2022 in .357Sig with two hundred rounds of ammunition on hand. He had only recently added a Ruger 22/45, twenty-two caliber pistol to his meager collection, and had paid a premium for a brick of five hundred rounds of .22Long Rifle ammunition for it.

9

The apartment complex he lived in was relative quiet through the rest of the day and through the night as people just stayed in or near their apartments waiting for their loved ones to return home by whatever manner they could find. Those that had propane or charcoal grills shared them to prepare meals since the stoves within the apartments were electric. Kevin had a two burner Coleman stove with a twenty-pound gas bottle he used when off fishing over a weekend and he cooked his meals outside since there was no ventilation in the apartment. He shared his stove with the lady and her two kids next door as she was scared and waiting for her husband to return home.

Kevin insured his bathtub was clean then filled it with water because he was sure that once the water towers drained to a point, they might not refill unless the electric pumps were able to function. He also advised his neighbor to do the same and if possible, gather water from the apartment complex's swimming pool for the toilet and bathing. Save the water in the tub for drinking and cooking.

As he moved around the complex, Kevin wore his Sig under an old camouflage hunting shirt just in case things began to turn sour. The two police officers that lived in the complex had removed their uniforms and just watched for the more violent criminal activity especially since several people from the complex had returned pushing baskets of food and bottled water from the Walmart store three blocks away. Just after one in the morning, Kevin entered the Walmart with his empty field pack and a medium size duffle and raided the store. He nearly filled the duffle with boxes of the twelve pack Noodles Ramen which he emptied each carton to save room in the duffle. Packaged, precooked foods came next along with a couple containers of salt and pepper. Cracker type foods such as peanut butter and crackers were also dumped into his duffle then once he filled it up he moved onto the energy food bars putting them into his field pack.

He emptied boxes of Nutrisystem meal boxes into his pack knowing they were also precooked and could be heated in a pot or pan over a small fire later if needed. Four bottles of Aleve and some first aid items then he moved to camping, and gathered up several camouflage patterned nylon tarps. Cans of Sterno finished his gathering trip and he was careful as he left the building as there were others also moving about inside gathering food. He had a thought and decided to risk involvement with the others and went back and took two boxes of powdered milk for his neighbor's kids.

Just after daylight he gave his neighbor, Mrs. Davenport, sixty packets of Noodles Ramen and the powdered milk. He advised her to block the patio doors at the rear of the apartment the best she could and helped her move her couch in front of it. Her kids were ages five and three and she was scared since her husband had yet to make it home. Kevin grabbed a couple hours sleep then cleaned out his cabinets of anything Mrs. Davenport might need in food that he was not prepared to haul off when he left the complex.

That night he made one more raid to Walmart for fuel for his camp stove which he was prepared to give to Mrs. Davenport when he left. He returned with two twenty-pound bottles of propane and a few sundry items then rested. After he awoke he began to pack and repack his field pack for the trip he was planning to return to his family farm and his parents.

On afternoon of the seventeenth, there was a knock on his door. He looked through the security peephole to see the little brunette from across the parking lot standing at his door looking worn. He opened the door to see her standing in jeans and a tank top with her hair a mess and looking as if she had not slept in days. Kevin had seen her several times at the apartment complex swimming pool in bikini's that showed off her body but today she was not the attractive woman he would have liked in his bed.

"Mister Barnes, do you have any food you could share with me. I'll let you fuck me if you have some food I could have."

"When was the last time you ate?"

"Yesterday. Please, I'll do anything for some food."

"Stay right there, let me look."

Kevin closed the door as he went to his pantry. He had been boxing up his can goods to give to his neighbor but had set four cans of chili aside since he felt it would not be good for the children with the spices the chili contained. He gathered them up then grabbed one of the manual can openers out of a drawer before returning to the door.

"What is your name?"

"Marissa, my name is Marissa. Is that for me?"

"Yes, Marissa it is, but first, on your knees."

"On my knees? Here, outside your apartment?"

"If you want the cans, get on your knees."

She dropped to her knees and knew what he expected her to do and she did just that. When she finished she put him back as he was, wiped her mouth and stood up. He handed her the cans and can opener before she ran back to her apartment. Kevin thought to himself she was very talented, but he honestly did not enjoy that as much as he would have a week earlier. He returned to his packing and within an hour he was knocking on his neighbor's door with a box of food in his arms.

"Mrs. Davenport, its Kevin, open the door, I have some food for you."

She opened the door to the safety chain and peeked out, then closed the door to release the chain and opened it so he could enter with the box of food.

"Mrs. Davenport, I'm leaving here tonight. I have two more boxes of food in my apartment for you and I think I'll just

12

leave my key in front of your door and you can get the food as you want it. I'll bring the stove over in a few minutes, so you do not have to mess with it. Just be careful and keep the tank is turned off when not being used."

"Thank you, Kevin. You've been a good neighbor. Hopefully Gary will be home tonight or tomorrow."

"I hope so too but maybe you should think about getting yourself and the kids out of this place before you find yourself trapped."

"I wouldn't know where to go. We are from Memphis and hardly know anyone except the people here in the complex."

"I understand. I'd take you and the kids with me but the journey I have planned is going to be hard enough on me, I'd hate to think about how it would be on your or the kids."

"I understand Kevin. Thank you again."

Kevin smiled and turned back to her door to leave.

"Kevin, I saw what you did with that Smith girl from across the parking lot. I hope I never get that desperate to have to humiliate myself in such fashion."

"I hope you don't have to either but sadly it may come to that to feed your kids. I'm sorry but I cannot stay and protect you, I must go. I have family to check on that may need me."

"I understand Kevin. Thank you."

Kevin moved the stove into her apartment and made sure she knew how to use it before leaving with a wet kiss on his cheek. He had obtained the garden wagon used by the apartment complex grounds keeper and had it loaded with items that he felt he would need beyond what he had in his pack. Kevin was dressed and ready to leave at a moment's notice and took a nap as he waited until he felt it would be safe to leave. His wind-up alarm woke him at fifteen minutes before midnight and he carefully left his apartment and listened for sounds of movement around the complex. Ten minutes later he pulled the wagon out of his apartment and set out on his journey with his AK hanging in front of him ready to use.

He knew he could average three miles an hour with a standard pack load, but he was heavier than normal plus he was pulling the wagon which he was glad it rolled with ease under its load. Kevin had left nearly four hours later than he would have like to get clear of the major portion of the city and even part of the early morning once out into the country. But right now, he was more concerned about what was moving in the darkness and moved slowly to insure he did not walked into something he could not deal with. He was wishing he had his night vision goggles he wore when training at night but the yellow lensed wrap-around glasses he was wearing helped brighten his surroundings as the half-moon gave some light to assist his journey.

Kevin checked his watch as the terrain opened from city to the urban area surrounding the city and figured he had about an hour before the sun would be up enough to give him away. He started looking for a place to hunker down for the day and found a field with grass that was over waist high. He moved around the edge of the barbed wire enclosed field until he found a gate. Using the bolt cutters from the wagon he cut the chain holding the gate closed, entered then used a zip tie to make it look as if the gate was still secure. He traveled down the dirt road for about two hundred meters before turning off into the grass for about twenty meters. Kevin watched the area well past daylight to insure he had not walked into someone's front yard as he ate an MRE.

Once he had finished eating and figured this was just a hay field, he rigged a cover from the wagon, crawled under it and went to sleep. He was awakened once by dogs barking close by, but they never came near enough for him to be concerned. Gunfire woke him a second time and he just lay still listening as another round of shooting seemed to move away from his location. His alarm finally woke him an hour before dark and he made coffee on his Sterno stove and ate before carefully moving out of his position onto the road then to the gate. He sat at the gate for almost twenty minutes before cutting the zip tie. Just as he cut it his bowels complained and he backed away from the gate, moved the wagon into the grass and quickly dropped his gear so he could void his bowels. He had six rolls of toilet paper in zip lock baggies and cleaned himself before once more putting his gear on then moving back to the gate.

Kevin had looked at his map of the county he had used as he traveled from one handyman job to another while he was eating and had determined he had traveled eleven miles that night. Tonight, he hoped to do better since he was out of the city, but because it was still early, he took his time. One thing to his benefit was at this time in history, humanity was still tied to the light and coverage once darkness fell. He knew a certain element preferred the darkness to do their evil, but the farther away from the city the less likely he would run into that portion of humanity.

April 19th

Leaving

It was nearly midnight when he heard shots being fired in a suburb he was passing near on one of the back roads. As he came closer to the housing area he heard a woman screaming in the distance and then minutes later the laughter of men as those cries became quieter. He thought of Mrs. Davenport but knew he could not have protected her for long or that she and the kids could have kept up with him even at the slow pace he was taking. He put that out of his mind and moved on. An hour later when he stopped to take a short break, he looked back towards the housing area and saw flames over the trees as the place was on fire.

Kevin found a place just at daylight to make camp and was glad to have the pack off his aching back. He estimated he had done almost twenty-one miles during the night and as he ate an MRE he realized that he did not remember a lot of that distance he had traveled. Sleep came quick, but the slightest sounds woke him up as he had to admit to himself he was scared of something or someone finding him asleep.

He woke tired, ate and refilled his water bladder from a gallon jug he had in the wagon then once more started out for his parent's home.

On the third night, he was making decent time as he had moved into open farmland on the back roads which would ultimately take him to his parent's farm. He heard a shot as he approached a farmhouse set back off the road and stopped, moving his wagon off the road and just waited as he listened for any other shots or noise which might bring danger to him. Less than ten minutes later her heard two men laughing and talking as they approached his position. As they came closer, he heard one man comment on how that old woman screamed when he shoved his

16

cock into her ass as they raped her. In Kevin's mind, he saw his mother being raped, then Mrs. Davenport and even the Smith girl. He just could not allow that any more women be hurt by these men.

Kevin stepped out into the road and before either man could react, he killed them. Two rounds each, center mass chest as he had been taught in Infantry school. The one hundred and twenty-four grain jacket hollow points in his AK-47 at about twenty yards ripped through the men's chests, killing them almost immediately. Kevin had been shot at in Afghanistan and had fired back at men, but he never knew if his bullets connected with a body over there since things often moved so fast and other people were often shooting at the same human target. He stood for a moment with his rifle pointed at the bodies on the ground before the shakes began to take over his body.

The only sounds he could hear was the ringing in his ears of his own muzzle blasts and a few birds making noise in the tree line. When he got control of his shakes he walked over to the bodies and using a red lensed flashlight looked at them closer. Both men were dressed in a hunter's camouflage clothing and needing a shave. He could also smell their body odor as they had not cleaned themselves for some days. Both were carrying handguns and one had an AR-15 while the other had a Winchester Model 94 lever action. They also had large duffle type bags on their backs. Kevin drug one then the other man off the road and began stripping them of any usable items.

Inside the duffle bags he found clothing, jewelry and food. In the men's pockets, he found money and other items most likely stolen from the people they assaulted. One pistol was a cheap 9mm Highpoint while the other was a Kimber 1911A1 in 45ACP. He kept the Kimber and tossed the Highpoint out into the weeds after stripping the magazines of the ammunition. The rifles and their ammunition went into his wagon along with the food stuffs and knives.   He left the bodies with their clothes cut apart and moved down to the house they had come from.

Kevin found the woman of the house naked on a bed lying on her stomach with blood around her anus and a bullet hole in the back of her head. Her husband was in the kitchen with his head half blown off lying on the floor. The house had been ransacked. Kevin looked towards the rear of the house from the back door towards the barn and figured his time before daylight. He moved into the barn and after covering the wagon with bales of hay, he moved into the loft and went to sleep after stringing wires across both barn doors to trip anyone trying to enter while he was asleep. He woke in the late afternoon and took a bath in the cattle tank near the barn after cleaning the floating debris out of it. Before he left, he searched the kitchen one last time for any food items that he could use and waited until dark to leave the farm. Any weapons he found in the house he took out to the water tank and tossed them in along with any ammunition he could not use. He did keep a Smith & Wesson Model 25 revolver which was chambered in 45 Colt along with seventy rounds of ammunition. As he turned out of the driveway, he heard coyotes snarling and barking near where he had left the bodies. He smiled and moved away from the farm.

April 22nd

Home Coming

Four days after he had left his apartment, he sat on the wagon in the middle of the road across from the entrance to his parent's farm waiting until the sun was up. His plan was once the sun was up to walk down his parent's driveway, so they would know it was him returning home. He was exhausted but at least his destination was in sight. The sun was up for nearly an hour before he forced himself off the wagon and started the last three hundred yards of his journey.

Kevin stopped in front of the house and yelled to his parents. The second time he yelled the front door opened and his father stepped out with his rifle in his hands. It only took a moment for his father to recognize him and lowered the rifle as Kevin walked to him and upon the porch. It was a tearful reunion for them especially when his father told him his mother had been killed the day before by a man trying to steal food. His father took Kevin to the grave he had dug for his mother and the steel plate grave marker on it. Kevin asked about the man who had killed her, and he was told the man was lying out in the south pasture for the coyotes and buzzards to dine on.

The farm used propane for heat and cooking. Electricity for the wells pump was provided by a decades old generator that his father had maintained which did not have any electronics to be crippled by the EMP burst. He had only been using the generator one hour a day to insure the small water tower was full and the deep freezer for the meats was kept cool enough to store the food kept inside of it. While showering, his father fixed him steak and eggs before telling him to lay down and rest after his long night on the road. Kevin laid down in his old bed and immediately fell asleep.

The next week was taken up with watching for people who were moving out of the cities into the country looking for food while doing the minimum of chores to keep the farm functional. Kevin discovered that there was a large amount of preserved food in the basement which his mother had either prepared or purchased after they had been snowed in for two weeks while he was in Afghanistan.

Kevin strung barbed wire across the entrance to the driveway to slow down or prevent people from just walking up to the house. He had also laid wire in the grass along the road frontage just inside the fences so if someone crossed a fence would get tangled up and given the idea that they were not to be trespassing. Twice they were shot at by people who determined they could not easily enter the farm before they moved on down the road to find food or shelter elsewhere. His father told him he had not had any contact with is neighbors since the event but from time to time gunfire could be heard from the directions of the other small farms in the area.

After they found a cow that had been shot and partially butchered, they decided it might be time to vacate the farm and try to head for the mountains and Kevin's Uncle Henry's place. The old Ford tractor would run and pull a wagon for supplies, but it was too slow and would require a lot of fuel. There was also the old Dodge Power Wagon truck that they had rebuilt several years ago but it would attract a lot of attention day or night. It was decided to build pack frames for the horses and use them to transport supplies. They would ride at night and hunker down during the day with two horses for supplies. It was a good plan until a group of men came up through the east pasture after cutting several fences raiding for food.

Kevin was in the barn when he heard shooting. He grabbed his AK and ran to the house in time to see his Father fall from a bullet in his chest. Kevin engaged the men spread out on the lawn in front of the house and the fight lasted for less than five minutes but left Kevin with a flesh wound to his leg and his father dead. After he buried his father next to his mother, Kevin tied the five dead raiders to the tractor and drug them up to the entrance of the drive and left them for anyone passing by to see.

Smoke filled the sky to the East as the city was burning. Smoke to the north told him a farm was on fire. Kevin finished making the cradles for the horses, then went through the packaged food to find the foods he could easily pack, and the horses would not be too heavily burdened. Clothes, a couple of tarps and ropes for shelter when needed and other essentials for life were selected and packed. He had to smile at how his mother had prepared for another long term stay on the farm without being able to leave. She had always been the planner in the family and practical in her methods.

His father had a first-generation night vision scope mounted on a Winchester in .243 caliber for shooting coyotes at night. Kevin packed it with all the ammunition available plus the rechargeable batteries for the scope. A roll-up solar panel to recharge the batteries was added to the pile of gear he was taking. The last things he loaded were his father's Smith & Wesson Model 28-1 with all the .357 Magnum ammunition in the house along with the .410 single shot shotgun with fifty rounds of ammunition.

Kevin sealed up all the important papers of the family plus a lot of the family photos in plastic then buried them in the event he survived and returned to the farm to claim it as his own property. He then disabled any of the equipment that would function such as the tractor and Dodge Power Wagon. The last thing he did was rig up simple devices to set the house, barn and out buildings on fire once he was clear of the property. He was not going to give anything to anyone out there to use to survive or for shelter. Just at dark, he set the fuses on the devices, climbed into the saddle of his father's gelding and rode west, cutting fences as he needed until he felt it was safe to take to the road. An hour later he looked back to see the glow of his family's farm on fire. That was the last time he looked back. He was looking forward, to the West and hopefully Uncle Henry's place to ride this storm out.

Over a decade earlier, his father and a couple of neighbors hit on the idea of operating a wagon train tour for city folks who wanted to experience the early life on the prairies. He had all the Geological Survey maps from that time which would take him to the foothills of the Rockies. At best, he figured it would take him two months to reach his Uncle Henry's place.

****

Journal entry, May 3rd.

I'm keeping this journal for a couple of reasons. First is to somewhat record my experiences as I travel to Uncle Henry's place in Colorado. It will also help me keep track of time. I probably won't make a daily entry, but I will try to at least notate the date, so I can track my time.

Since leaving my apartment, I have killed six men. No doubt that the first two deserved to die after what they had done to an elderly couple. The next four died along with my father in what was probably a search for food. I can only hope that I can avoid having to kill again but from what I have seen and have been hearing in the distance, the odds are against me.

In a few minutes I will set the fires to burn my parent's farm to the ground, so no one can benefit from their hard work. I'm only taking about a fourth of the food stuffs and gear available to me, but I don't want to stress the horses. If I can supplement what I have with game off the land, I can make it to Colorado if I am careful.

More later.

* * * * * * * * * *

Journal Entry, May 5th.

It's been nearly a month since the bombs went off and all I have had to do is think while riding West.

I had that girl at the apartments blow me before I gave her food and now I can say that was wrong of me. A couple days later I killed two men who had raped a woman according to their statements as they talked walking down a road. I killed them thinking about the people I left behind that had no protection, but I did not force the girl to blow me, just made her the offer and she took it. She offered her body to me for food and I took her mouth instead.

I find no remorse in killing those two murderers/rapist on the road to my folks place any more than I feel remorse for the four men I killed that killed my father.

I can only hope that I don't have to kill any more people before I get to Uncle Henry's place, but I have a feeling the killing will go on. Even as I write this, I can hear gun fire off in the distance. I can only be grateful that it is so far away.

* * * * * * * * * *

May 17th

A Lost Child

For two weeks, Kevin traveled back roads and cut fences, traveling through pastures and wheat fields as major cities and towns fell behind him. Once he was clear of enough of populations, he changed to traveling during the day, so he could make better time. He was traveling through farm and ranch land doing everything he could to avoid any level of population. Kevin was being cautious not to over stress the horses since they carried the things he needed to make the journey to his uncle's place far off in the mountains.

Kevin kept his binoculars at hand to search as far ahead as possible, looking for signs of activity while looking for places to water the horses and even camp for the evening. He would take care of the horses at each stop before he took care of himself. Checking to insure each horse was not developing any sores on their back insured he could travel without worrying about if one of the horses would be difficult to handle or become useless for his needs.

He passed several farms within viewing range that appeared burned. Crops were growing in many of the fields but who was going to harvest them if the scavengers destroyed the means to harvest them or killed the people who had the knowledge to grow and harvest them. The people moving out of the cities in search for food were the true zombies of the world. He came across the carcasses of cattle that had been killed and partially butchered on site only removing what a person could carry while leaving the bulk of the meat to ruin on the ground.

Kevin found a nice area along a creek to spend a couple days to allow the horses to rest as he also rested. Shooting could be heard in the distance from the direction he had traveled, and he watched that path to insure he was not being followed. He did catch movement along the creek to his south, but it appeared to be a single individual, not a group. Kevin moved to a position further down the creek and finally caught sight of a single small person moving up the creek bottom towards his camp. It was a child of indeterminate age and sex, but he suspected it was a girl due to the length of hair.

When he was sure she was alone, he moved back to his camp and just sat down, pouring a cup of coffee warming on the coals of his small campfire. He tried not to be obvious as he watched her move closer to his camp until she ran out of brush to hide behind and just watched him until he finally called out to her.

"Are you going to sit out there all day waiting for me to leave or go to sleep?"

She stood and walked slowly into his camp, stopping about twenty feet away watching him as he just sat and sipped on his coffee.

"Mister, I'll let you rape me if I can have something to eat."

"What's your name and how old are you?"

"Amanda Spencer and I'm twelve. Mister, I haven't had any real food in days and I'm hungry."

"Well Amanda, you are too young for me to rape as you have offered, and I will give you some food, but you have to do one or two things for me first."

"What do I need to do for something to eat?"

Kevin slowly stood and moved to his saddlebags, retrieved a bar of soap and washcloth then handled them out to her.

"Take a bath in the creek. I can smell you from over here and it is neither a pleasant smell nor a healthy one for you. Wash your body then your clothes and I will find something for you to wear while your clothes dry."

She just stood looking at him.

"Listen Amanda, I will not harm you. I prefer my sexual partners a lot older than you are. No bath, no food. It's your choice."

Amanda looked down at his campfire at the small skillet sitting next to it then at the bags sitting around the camp with his possessions in them. She moved to him where she could reach out and take the soap and washcloth from his hand and then moved back away from him towards the creek bank. Kevin sat back down as he watched her removed her clothes. She had sores on her body that were angry and red needing treatment which most likely came from insect bites. Amanda walked out into the creek and began scrubbing herself as he moved to one of the packs and found the plastic box with Bag Balm ointments normally used on the animals on the farm which worked very well on humans.

Watching her, Kevin remembered another twelve-year-old girl and a creek much like this one. Skinny dipping with Gwendolyn was one of his fondest memories of growing up. It was on that same creek bank on his sixteenth birthday she gave herself to him after a dip in the creek. By age eighteen she had moved on to an older man and the last time Kevin saw her nearly a year ago, she was pregnant with their second child. He shook off those memories and continued looking for things he would need to take care of the girl.

In another pack, he found scissors then walked over and removed the horse's mane comb from his saddlebag. He walked over to the creek bank and watched as she washed herself and shivered in the cool water. Kevin told her to wash between her legs really well, and the crack of her butt. He told her to wash her hair twice as it transformed from a dirty brown to a dark blond. He also made her bend over and spread her butt cheeks, so he could

26

insure she was clean and had her wash again as he went back to his bags, found talcum powder and a large towel.

When she thought she was clean enough, she left the creek and stood shivering waiting for him to make his move. Kevin had her turn around and told her he was going to cut her hair. Once it was cut and combed the best he could as he was careful not too pulled too hard on the tangles in it he had her go back and wash her hair again. Privately he was surprised she did not have lice considering her condition. Once he approved of her washing he told her to dry off before he treated her insect bites and such.

Once dry, he had her bend over and spread her butt cheeks as he sprinkled talcum power to ease the rawness he could see from not being able to properly clean herself when voiding her bowels. He moved her closer to the campfire and carefully put ointment on the angry places where she had suffered insect bites. She shivered with every touch of his fingers and he detached himself of the fact she was completely exposed to him. Once he had finished, he handed her the talcum powder and told her to carefully powder her vagina as he went to another bag and found sweatshirt for her to wear.

Kevin had spread out a saddle blanket for her to sit on as she waited for him to fix her something to eat. It took him a minute to find a package of backpacker's oatmeal for her. A cup of Orange drink mix from his MRE's was added to her first meal with him. She cried as he handed her the cup with the orange drink and he warned her not to drink it too fast. When he handed her the oatmeal he once more warned her not to eat too fast since she had been without regular food for a while. She did as she was told as he just sat and watched her eat. When she had scraped every bit of oatmeal from the metal bowl, she sat it aside and looked at him before lying back on the blanket and spreading her legs.

"What are you doing Amanda? I told you that you were too young for me to have sex with. Now sit up and listen to me."

She sat up and straightened the sweatshirt to once more hide her vulnerable parts from him.

"I'm going to rig a clothes line and after that small meal has a chance to settle in your stomach, you are going to wash your clothes in the creek and hang them on the line to dry along with the washcloth and towel. But you will have to remove the sweatshirt as you do that but leave it on the blanket, so it does not get wet or dirty. Understand?"

"Yes Sir."

"Amanda, my name is Kevin Barnes. You can call me Kevin to keep things simple."

"Okay Kevin."

As he rigged the clothesline, he asked her how she came to be out here alone. She told him her parents were divorced and when things became bad in the city her mother took her and her fourteen-year-old sister away in search of safety. They had been wandering for nearly a month before her mother and sister were caught by some men. She had gone into the woods to pee and found some blackberries and was picking them when she heard her mother scream. Soon both her mother and sister were screaming, and she ran back to their camp but stopped before being seen by the men. They were raping her mother and sister. There were five men and they all took turns with them and she knew she would be next if they caught her, so she ran. That was about two weeks ago, and she had been living on berries and anything else that did not make her sick.

Amanda said she did see her mother and sister being led off by those men later with ropes around their necks. She had seen other men since then but had avoided them. When Kevin asked why she came to him, she said she had seen him riding in and thought maybe he was different. Kevin then asked her why she was willing to give her body to him if she thought he was different from the other men, she told him it was all she had to offer in payment for the food and she had reached the point where it no longer mattered to her as long as she could eat.

Kevin tended to the horses then had her wash her clothes. He made sure they were rinsed well then, he hung each item up as she washed the next. She told him she had to pee once, and he told her to just pee in the creek. She gave him an odd look then squatted, did her business then went back to work washing her tattered shirt. Before she got out of the creek he had her splash water up onto her vagina to insure no urine remained then he handed her the towel as she exited. He hung the towel up as she put the sweatshirt back on and sat back down on the saddle blanket.

Amanda asked him where he was going, and he told her. He then told her if she wanted, she could go with him until he found a place civilized where she would not be used as a whore, but she would have to help around the camp doing chores such as washing the dishes and such after each meal. She thought about his offer for a while and then told him she had no place to go so going with him was better than wandering the woods waiting to starve to death. Amanda made one more offer to give herself to him in payment and he scolded her for such a thought.

She laid back down on the blanket on her side and fell asleep. Kevin wondered if this was a smart move to take her along, but he had to admit to being lonely and another hand, even a young one would be helpful. Cleaned up she had all the appearance of a young girl who could grow up to be a lovely woman. Maybe it was his mother's influence or the effect of seeing young girls used in Afghanistan as property, but he could not think of her as anything except someone needing help. He thought about how desperate she must have felt as she offered her body to him just for something to eat. How many females were doing just that at the moment just to stay alive? The world had become barbaric once more.

Kevin knew whatever was left of the government had to be working on putting things back in order, but the damage was done. What he was not aware of was that war was raging all along the coasts as Muslim's were fighting Christian's and anyone else that would not bow their necks to their rule. The American fleets that were at sea returned to add their support, but it was bitter fighting in the major cities along racial and religious lines. Further out it was between those that had and those that wanted what the others had.

That evening he fixed Amanda the rest of the oatmeal for her supper. Kevin had developed a routine where he would open a packet designed for two people and eat half for breakfast and the other half for supper restricting himself to two meals a day. He was going to do the same with Amanda for the time being, especially feeding her softer foods to allow her stomach to catch back up with eating. Kevin gave her his sleeping bag for the night and had her strip before going to sleep. In the morning, he had her just stand still, nude before him as he checked her sores and reapplied ointment on them before allowing her to dress with her rear and vagina powdered up.

* * * * * * * * *

Journal Entry, May 17th

Well I am no longer alone now. Amanda Spencer, a 12 years old girl wandered into my camp and offered her body to me to sexually use for something to eat. I made her wash her body in the creek I'm camped by and for a moment, I envision an old love as we used to skinny dip in a creek and later made love next to it when we were 16. Amanda is ate up with bug bites, and she had a rash in her pubic and ass.

Even if she wasn't malnourished and covered in bug bites, I would never take what she was offering. But I would be lying to myself if for a second, and only a second it was tempting to accept her offer.

I wonder how many girls her age was being used in such a fashion now just, so they can survive in this upside-down world?

* * * * * * * * *

Kevin decided to stay one more day and showed her how to take care of the horses. She was scared at first but realized they were gentle and well mannered. He cut the sleeves off the sweatshirt, so she could wear it without the long, bulky sleeves getting in the way as she did the few chores needed to be done each day. He hunted for squirrels during the day and that night they ate hot meat instead of dipping into the packaged rations. He showed her how to clean the dishes and inspected them only having her wash one a second time explaining that if not clean they could become ill.

He made her bath again then after he had taken care of her sores and had her apply a bit of ointment on her rash around her vagina, she handed him the soap and told him to take a bath. He laughed and stripped to his birthday suit and bathed as she watched him as he had watched her telling him to wash his butt again. She was laughing as she spoke then went to clean around the camp as he finished washing and dried off. He put on clean clothes and put his dirty clothes in a bag separate from his clean ones telling her the next time they camped for a couple days he would wash them, but they were leaving in the morning and they might not dry overnight.

May 20th

Temporary Refuge

Two days later Kevin scanned a farm house set well off the road looking for any movement telling him to avoid the area. There were vehicles parked in front of the house and the farm equipment looked maintained. For an hour, he looked for any sign of life around the house without finding any. There were horses out in the pasture near the barn and a few head of cattle in the same pasture. The fields surrounding the house were green with wheat growing about a foot high. Amanda had been riding behind him as there was no place comfortable for her to ride with the packs on the other horses. They rode down to the barn and he left Amanda with the horses with orders to stay out of sight if shooting started. He carefully checked the barn before moving to the house.

Kevin moved to the house as if he was moving on an enemy position with his AK up and pointing to where he was heading. At the back door, he noticed it was closed but had not been kicked open. Carefully he turned the doorknob, but the door was locked. He looked back at the barn and saw Amanda standing just inside by the door. He motioned that he was going around the house and she waved that she understood. He was careful as he moved around the house peeking in windows to see if there was any movement inside the house. Kevin was nervous as he moved onto the large front porch with the AK shoulder and ready for action. The front door was also locked.

He looked towards the attached garage noticing the doors were closed and thought for a minute realizing there was no farm truck to be seen. Kevin went back around the back of the house and kicked in the back door and moved quickly into the mud room and then into the kitchen. Slinging the AK behind his back he drew his pistol and began to inspect the house, room by room until he was certain it was vacant. Just before he moved to exit through the kitchen he thought about if there was a basement. He found the basement door and slowly went down into it with his pistol ready and a flashlight to guide his way. It was void of human life, dead or alive. Kevin breathed a sigh of relief and went back upstairs and motioned to Amanda to come to the house.

Amanda found Kevin at the desk in the living room going through mail and such trying to figure out why the house was locked up and undisturbed. Finally, he found a copy of an entry form to a cattle show in Dodge City for the very same day of the event. Looking at photos and trophies in the house told him they had gone to the cattle show and were caught one hundred and fifty-eight miles from home. If they were going to make it home, they should have been back by now.

"Amanda, see if you can find some clothes to wear. These folks are gone and most likely will never be back. Also see if any of the shoes or boots will fit you."

"Okay Kevin." And she went to the bed rooms to do as she was told. A few minutes later she came out into the hall and spoke loud enough for him to hear her.

"Kevin, these are all boy's clothes."

"I know Amanda, but see if anything will fit you. You need clothes before those rot off your body. Now go try them on to include underwear."

A few minutes later she startled Kevin when she spoke right behind him.

"Kevin, these panties feel weird."

Kevin turned around to see her standing naked except for wearing a pair of boy's BVD's. He tried not to laugh but his smile probably gave him away.

"Amanda those are not panties, those are briefs or shorts for a boy. They are a little fuller in front because of a boy's penis and scrotum. Turn around." She turned around for him and he figured the shorts would do until they could find a place to obtain her some proper panties. Once she had made a complete turn and was looking back at him he spoke. "Amanda, they will do, now go put on a shirt and stop running around like we are lovers. It's one thing to have to see you bath in the creek and treat your cuts and scrapes but this is not acceptable. Go try on more clothes."

The next time she came into the living room she was wearing a clean t-shirt and a clean pair of jeans. Kevin checked out the fit on the jeans and told her a belt would keep them up until she gained a bit more weight. As she was trying on clothes, Kevin went through the house opening windows to help get the musty smell from the house and cool it down some. Once the house was open, he told her to keep trying on clothes and shoes while he went back to the barn to take care of the horses.

When he entered the house, Amanda was in the kitchen laying out food stuffs on the table. She was wearing high tops sneakers, jeans, a plain blue t-shirt, and a boy's camouflaged hunting vest. Hanging on her right hip was a full-size Buck Sheath Knife. Kevin just smiled as she went about sorting the items on the table and going back and forth from the cabinets and pantry to the table.

"Kevin, we have a lot of food here. Will the stove work?"

Kevin noticed the stove was gas and he remembered there was a propane tank behind the house. He opened the valve on a burner and it lit up with a nice blue flame.

"Kiddo, we are eating well tonight for sure. Let me find a source for water and we may stay a couple days before moving on."

Kevin went back outside and found the water well that supplied the house and barn. Inside the well house was a small Honda generator. He fueled the generator from gasoline he found in the well house and after several hard pulls on the starter rope, the generator kicked over and ran. Being in a cement block building with a tin roof must have protected any electronics contained within the generator. He shut it down and looked on how to tie it into the well pump. The farmer had a pigtail rigged for emergencies and within a couple minutes, Kevin had the well working again. He went into the house and after a minute, fresh water was flowing into the kitchen sink.

He went into the basement and found the hot water tank and saw the farmer had shut off the main burner but had left the pilot light on. He put it into heat mode and within a moment he heard the burner fire up and knew that within an hour they would have hot water. Kevin then went out to the propane tank to check on volume and found it to be half full. More than enough to last them a couple days.

Kevin spent the rest of the day going through the house room by room searching for anything they might use on their journey as Amanda cleaned the kitchen and continued to sort out the food items. She found an oil lamp and had Kevin light it for her, so she could go down into the basement to see what might be stored down there. She found a sleeping bag and other camping items which she brought up and put in the living room for her to use instead of sleeping in Kevin's sleeping bag.

During his search, Kevin found a gun safe inside a closet in the master bedroom. It was a simple key locked safe except the locked were concealed in a manner that they could not be easily accessed. After an hour of searching the master bedroom he found the keys hanging from a nail inside another closet above the door. On one side of the safe was shelves with cartridges for the firearms on the other side and hanging from the door. Kevin smiled as he found firearms that Amanda could easily handle and defend herself with. Now he just had to teach her how to safely use them.

Kevin called Amanda into the master bedroom and showed her the firearms lying on the bed. The pistol was a Ruger Mark II and the rifle was a Ruger 10-22. He told her he was going to teach her how to use them for her own protection and how to safely carry them. She looked at them for a moment before speaking.

"My Mother hated guns. She said they should all be banned but if she had had a gun then maybe my sister and her would not have been raped and led off like cattle."

She reached down and picked up the pistol and looked at it, being careful how she held it.

"If you will not use me that way then no man will use me unless I want them too. Yes, Kevin, teach me how to use these weapons to protect myself."

"I will, starting tomorrow. Right now, it's getting late and we need to eat and take a shower before it gets too dark. I don't want any lights in the house to alert someone from a distance that we are here."

They fixed a pot of Dinty Moore stew for dinner and a pitcher of Kool-Aid Fruit Punch to wash it down with. Crackers were available and afterwards, they each had a piece of Werther's Original candy for dessert found in a covered bowel in the living room. After the dishes were done, Amanda asked if she could have a bubble bath tonight. Kevin told her she could, and she took the oil lamp into the master bath and ran a tub of hot water with lots of bubble bath and just soaked in it until it started to cool. She dried herself off, brushed her hair with the brush she found on the bathroom counter and wrapped the towel around her and went back into the kitchen where she dropped the towel.

"Kevin, you need to put some ointment on my bites and make sure my rash is healing up."

Kevin was caught off guard by this but recovered enough to have her turn around and bend over to inspect the rash that she had around her anus. He told her to put some baby powder on it that he saw in the bathroom and then put on some panties while he went out to the barn to get the ointment. When he returned she was standing in the kitchen with the boy's briefs on but otherwise naked before him with a large butcher knife in her hand. He treated her bites then she put on the dark t-shirt she had brought into the kitchen. She told him it was his turn to clean up and she just sat down at the table opposite of him and poured herself another glass of fruit punch.

He looked in the bathroom mirror realizing he had not shaved since leaving the farm and took time to use the farmer's razor to remove his beard. He left his mustache, other than trimming it, then took a long hot shower. His hair was getting longer, and he considered cutting it but right now all he wanted to do was get cleaned up then bed. After he showered he found sweatpants and a t-shirt in the farmer's dresser that fit him well enough, then joined Amanda in the kitchen. She smiled as he walked in to the room.

"You look nice without the beard Kevin."

"Thank you and you look nice with your hair brushed out but I think I butchered your hair a bit when I first cut it so before we leave, I'll try to fix the mess I made of it."

They sat and talked about what they needed to do tomorrow. Teaching her to use the weapons was a priority then finding out if the horses on the farm were mild enough for her to ride so she would not have to ride behind him. Plus sorting out the food stuffs and hopefully at least one more horse to carry the additional load. Kevin lit another oil lamp and placed it into the common bathroom for her during the night. It was an interior room, so he felt there would be no light escaping to alert a passerby that someone was in the house. They moved the large

37

couch in the living room in front of the front door and he stacked pots and pans in front of the kitchen door to give them warning in case someone entered during the night.

* * * * * * * * *

Journal Entry, May 20th.

We got lucky today. We found an abandoned farm house with a nicely stocked pantry. Amanda has found clothes she can wear but she is having to wear boy's underwear since there does not seem to be any girls in this family. From what I can tell, the owners of this farm at stuck in Dodge City at a cattle show, otherwise we would not be here tonight.

* * * * * * * * *

Amanda took the butcher knife to the bedroom she was going to sleep in and Kevin told her if someone busted in during the night to get between the bed and wall and stay there until he came for her. And if she got up and left the room during the night to call out to him so he would know it was her in the house just in case they got in without making too much noise. They had been in bed less than an hour before Kevin was awakened by her calling out to him from the hallway. He sat up in bed with his pistol in his hand.

"Amanda, is everything alright?"

She walked into his room, put the butcher knife on his night stand and crawled into bed with him.

"I can't get to sleep. The house is making noises and it scares me."

"Yeah, houses do creak and moan at night. You normally don't notice it unless it is as quiet as it is. You can sleep with me but under a separate cover."

"Okay."

They quickly rearranged the covers and soon Kevin heard her breathing calm then a light snoring as she fell asleep. Kevin had a lewd thought that if she was five years older, then he would have no guilt in taking her. He shook that thought out of his head as he remembered who he was and who she was. Both victims of evil men's actions but that was not a good reason for him to have those thoughts. He made Marissa Smith blow him for food because she was old enough to have provided for herself as many of the young women in the apartment complex had, but she played on her looks to get by outside of her work. Amanda was a victim of her age and inability to protect herself. It was only sheer luck the men who took her mother and sister did not notice her before raiding their camp. He rolled over with his back to Amanda and fell asleep with an erection.

May 29th

Preparing to Move Again

They spent the next week working with the horses, finding a roan mare that was gentle for Amanda to ride and adjusting a saddle for her to use. She rode for an hour daily to get use to the mare and for the mare to get use to her. Amanda groomed the horse under Kevin's watchful eye after each riding session and he taught her the things to look for that might be a problem as she checked the mare's legs.

Instead of building frames for the horses, Kevin just saddled each one and rigged tie-downs, so they could attach packs and bags onto them, keeping the loads as light as possible and balanced. There was a single horse wagon in the barn that would have carried a large load, but two things crossed Kevin's mind as he considered it. First, he would have to handle the wagon which put him at a disadvantage while traveling, plus crossing creeks would be difficult. He had already crossed one river at a bridge and knew that any bridge would be a choke point for ambush unless they were very careful. The farther away from towns and cities long the country roads were still a risk but nothing like crossing even a small river bridge.

Amanda quickly learned how to use the firearms she would carry, and Kevin only had to scold her once when she mishandled the rifle, pointing it at him. He knew it was unloaded and the bolt was locked back to the rear, but she had to understand more people are shot with unloaded weapons than loaded ones. She carried the pistol in a nylon shoulder holster they found in the basement but the extra two magazines for it had to be carried in the hunting vest she had adopted as part of her clothing.

The rifle had a Bushnell scope on it that looked a lot like the tactical scopes used by the military with see-through mounts.

40

He taught her how to use the scope and the open sights on the rifle. Besides the two ten round magazines there were four twenty-five extended magazines for the rifle. She would carry the rifle with a twenty-five-round magazine, the two ten round mags would go into a vest pocket and they found a medium size shoulder bag for the other magazines and some other items for her to carry. He rigged the sling for the rifle, so she could carry it like he carried the AK in front of him ready to use or sling it behind her back out of the way.

Like a lot of farms and ranches out on the prairie where it might take an hour to drive to a grocery store, the farm's pantry was well stocked. Amanda spent her time away from her riding and shooting lessons repacking a lot of the food stuffs for easier packing and carrying. The Ramen Noodles she wrapped in aluminum foil to contain and protect them from moisture since their wrappers were so flimsy. A lot of the pre-cooked, microwave reheatables she just made sure they were protected then sat aside.

The basement had provided a treasure trove of items as it seemed the two boys on the farm were both Boy Scouts. Amanda built a pack under Kevin's guidance with a Sterno stove, a nice cook kit, plastic bowls and plates, plus a couple sets of eating utensils. Her clothing now consisted of four pairs of jeans, two pair of Boy Scout trousers, two pair of hiking boots, another pair of tennis shoes and numerous t-shirts and a dozen pair of boy's underwear. She had also added the combs and brushes from the master bath plus two packages of Kotex napkins since she knew she would probably start getting her period soon. Four flannel shirts and both a light jacket and a heavy coat for when the weather turned cold as they anticipated when they finally got to the Rockies, plus western style rain slicker for when they had rain upon them. Kevin added to his own clothing from the farmer's closet. The one item of clothing they both added was the hunter's camouflage clothing and jackets they found in the closets. This also provided Amanda with a floppy boonies style hat for her to wear.

Kevin hit pay dirt in the gun safe as there was a Remington Wing Master 12-gauge shotgun in it. There was a variety of loads for the shotgun including twenty rounds of 00 buckshot. He disassembled the shotgun, removing the plug restricting the amount of ammunition in the tube magazine, the carefully cut the barrel off just forward of the magazine with a pipe cutter he found in the equipment shed next to the barn. There was a rifle scabbard for attaching to a saddle in the barn and he modified it to carry the shotgun as he rode.

The days were busy as they prepared for their next step towards the mountains. Amanda slept with Kevin nightly but even as he treated her sores, she never again exposed herself to him. They showered nightly and Kevin finally released a bit of his sexual tension in the shower one night before going to bed.

They spent a total of nine days at the farm eating three meals a day and Kevin noticed Amanda was filling out now that she had a steady diet. They tried not to over eat at any specific meal but the morning they left, they all but stuffed themselves since they knew they would be back on two meals a day unless they found another place like this one.

* * * * * * * * * *

Journal Entry May 29th.

We're leaving the farm tomorrow. Amanda now has a horse to ride plus three more horses to help carry what we have found here. We have stripped this farm of everything we can carry and use.

Amanda is starting to fill out now that she has a steady diet. Even though she sleeps with me nightly under separate covers, I'm concerned that she is only doing that to allow me to use her instead of being scared as she claims. I have no idea of her motives are in doing so but she had not made any move to let me know that is why she wants to sleep with me.

Maybe I'm reading more into this than there is, but she is slowly becoming a distraction. At least she no longer exposes herself to me, so I can put ointment on her insect bites. She works hard to help me and seems to try not to be a bother. Maybe if she was at least 16. No, I need to get those thoughts out of my mind.

May 30th

A Friendly Kiss

Kevin was leading his original pack horses while Amanda was leading the three from the farm. The loads were distributed so if separated they both had food and protection from the elements separate from the other. The travel plan was simple in that they would ride for two hours, walk beside the horses for an hour then ride until a break at noon or at a creek or pond so the horses could water and rest even if they were still burdened by the loads. Kevin was keeping a sharp eye out at the horizon for anything that might be trouble as he was also looking for places to stop and rest.

Amanda also had a pair of binoculars and would from time to time look at their back trail to see if anyone might be following. The first night they camped at a pond, hobbled the horses and let them feed on the tall grass as they set up the small tent the boys had used and ate a modest meal. The tent was barely big enough for the two of them, but it was better than being exposed to any weather that might come in during the night. Amanda bathed in the pond, changed into clean underwear and went into the tent while Kevin bathed. That night she did something she had never done as she rolled over to Kevin, kissed him on the cheek before rolling back and going to sleep.

The next morning after they had everything ready to go, she walked up to him, pulled his head down to her and gave him a quick kiss on the lips. As she was walking away to her mare Kevin spoke up.

"Amanda what was that for?"

"That was for everything you have done for me and everything you have not done to me. I'm not trying to seduce you into anything you have already said you will not do, I just wanted

44

to show you how much I appreciate everything. Can't friends share a kiss from time to time without it being anything more than that?"

She turned back and walked to her mare and climbed into the saddle with a smile on her face as she looked at him. Kevin shook his head and mounted his gelding and they left the pond heading west. That night she had Kevin turn his back as she bathed, and she doctored the few remaining sores on her body, so he would not have to look at her or touch her. She kissed him on the cheek again before going to sleep.

* * * * * * * * *

Journal Entry, May 31st.

Amanda has upped her game. She is starting to give me little 'friendship' kisses but she is also making me look away as she bathes and as she is doctoring what's left of her sores. Even so it is hard to miss that she is filling out more now that she is eating better.

We're lucky to get 20 miles a day if that. Terrain and Amanda's inexperience with horses is part of the problem plus having to stop and cut so many fences is a problem, but at least she is not having to ride behind me, riding double. Plus, with 6 horses, it takes twice as long to unload and then load them as it did before. It's going to take longer now to get to Uncle Henry's, but at least we have rations and other things to help us make the trip.

June 5th

Changing Directions

They traveled for six days skirting a farm that had been burnt down and another that had smoke coming from the chimney before they found a large creek with a three-foot waterfall and camped there with plans to wash their dirty clothes and let the horses have a couple days rest. Amanda was hanging up her clothes to dry and when she finished she walked over to the campfire where Kevin was drinking a cup of coffee and poured herself a cup of orange drink from the small coffee pot they had brought from the farm for that use. As she was bent over she softly spoke to Kevin.

"We have company in the bushes down the creek."

"I know. Don't get between them and me."

Amanda moved around him and went to sit next to her saddle which had her rifle lying across it and just waited for Kevin to make a move when a call came from the bushes.

"Hello the camp!"

Kevin called out. "Enter and keep your hands where we can see them."

Kevin was watching the figure move from the bushes and recognized the green Marine digital uniform being worn by what appeared to be a woman. Amanda barely looked at the person as she was looking behind them to see if there was anyone else still hiding. The person stopped about twenty yards from Kevin and carefully removed the M-4 Carbine they had on a single point sling and laid it on the ground then removed the M9 Beretta from the holster on their vest, also laying it down next to the rifle. They pushed their floppy hat back off their head and removed the sunglasses they were wearing. The woman before them was black, moderately nice looking and sturdy built considering the vest and clothing hid her physical condition very well.

She pulled a set of dog tags from her uniform and held them away from her body as a form of identification.

"I'm Corporal Lavon Kincaid, United States Marine Corps. And who am I talking too?"

Kevin reached into his shirt and pulled out his dog tags for her to see.

"Sergeant Kevin Barnes, Army. This is my niece, Amanda Collins. What are you doing out here alone and where are you heading?"

"I was assigned as a clerk to the Marine Reserve unit in Cheyenne when this happened. When my commander realized it was all coming apart he kicked us loose to find our way either home or to a unit that was stable. I'm from Santa Fe and was trying to get back home until this settles down. I left with a male companion until four days ago when he left our camp only wearing his boots and ate a bullet. I saw you leave the other creek early this morning and I have been shadowing you figuring that you were not like some of the people I have come across since I left Cheyenne. I'm out of food and just plain tired."

"Where's the rest of your kit?"

"About a hundred meters back down the creek bottom."

"Go get it and bring it in. Amanda would you find something for the Corporal to eat please."

"Yes, Uncle Kevin." She said with a bit of humor in her voice.

Lavon turned to go get her gear and looked down at her rifle and pistol, then moved on without attempting to pick them up.

Kevin looked at Amanda who was smiling as she dug into the food bag for something to feed the Corporal. When Lavon was out of hearing Kevin spoke.

"What are you smiling at kiddo?"

"Well I seriously doubt she believes I am your niece from the look on her face when you called me your niece. Second, now you have someplace to put that erection you often go to sleep with if she is willing."

"Damn Amanda, I thought I raised you better than that!" But he had a smile on his face as he replied to her.

"Yes, Uncle dear, you did. Now play nice, she'll be back soon."

Lavon returned with two packs and a shoulder bag. Strapped to one bag was another M4 Carbine. She set them down next to her rifle and pistol and stepped towards the campfire when Amanda spoke.

"Corporal, when was the last time you bathed?"

"It's been a few days. Why?"

"First you take a bath in the creek, then you get to eat. You'll feel much better if you do."

Lavon looked at the smile on Kevin's face and the firm look on Amanda's then began to remove the vest then her uniform blouse. When in her t-shirt Kevin noticed she was nicely built, solid with modest breasts under what he figured was a sports bra. Amanda interrupted his viewing of Lavon as she sat down to remove her boots.

"Uncle Kevin, would you be a gentleman and go tend to the horses while the Corporal takes a bath before she eats?"

Kevin laughed and stood up picking his shotgun up as he did so.

"I most certainly will. Just holler when things are decent again."

Kevin climbed the creek bank and sat with his back to a tree looking away from the creek. Lavon stripped as Amanda got a bar of soap from her saddlebags and tossed it to her. Lavon walked out into the creek, sat down on the slab rock creek bottom and began to wash several days of dirt and sweat from her body. Amanda laid out a saddle blanket for her to sit on once out of the creek then placed a clean towel on the blanket for her to use. Lavon looked up at the creek bank noticing Kevin never turned to look at the events happening behind him. Even as cool as the water was, she had to admit it felt great to relax at bit as she got herself clean. She scrubbed her hair the best she could, then moved so she could lean back into the tiny waterfall and let it rinse the soap from her hair. When she sat up and began to get out of the water she was glad that he had not been watching because the cool water had caused her nipples to harden, standing out from her breasts.

Amanda asked her if she had any clean clothes to put on. Lavon responded that she didn't so Amanda went to Kevin's clothing bag, removed a pair of sweat pants and a t-shirt for her to wear until other arrangements could be made. Once dried off and clothed, Amanda called for Kevin to return to camp. Amanda served her a can of Campbell's Steak and Potato soup along with a cup of the orange drink.

Lavon told them between bites that they had limited communications with Headquarters in Washington and told about the reports of fighting in and around the capital. She also mentioned they received a rumor of cannibalism within the major cities since they were so isolated from food sources. When the fighting escalated in Cheyenne that was when they took MATV's and left the city. Their MATV broke down about a hundred miles from here and they had been walking ever since.

Kevin dug out a pair of running shorts for Lavon to wear as she washed her clothes. He rigged another line for her and Amanda hung them up as Lavon handed them to her. Kevin brought the horses down two at a time to water then back into the pasture to feed insuring they were securely hobbled. After the horses were tended to and Lavon's clothes were washed, he ran them out of the camp, so he could take a bath. The conversation between Lavon and Amanda got interesting while alone away from his hearing.

"So, Amanda, do you enjoy sleeping with Kevin at your age?"

"Lavon, if you mean him having sex with me, it has not happened despite my best efforts."

"Why at your age would you want to have sex? You're too young to appreciate it."

"Because it is all I really have to give him for saving my life."

Amanda went on to tell her about how they found each other and her willingness to let him rape her so she could have something to eat. She told Lavon about the bathing before eating and Lavon laughed since that is what Amanda had done to her. Amanda admitted that part of the reason she had slept with Kevin at the farm was because she hoped he would use her, not so much because she wanted to be used, but to ease her guilt at him taking care of her without asking much in return. Lavon asked Amanda if she loved Kevin which Amanda blushed and admitted she was in love with him now that she had got to know him better.

She then did something that shocked Lavon. Amanda reached into her jeans pocket and pulled out a condom and handed it to her.

"Here, do me a favor and have sex with him. I've seen him go to sleep too many times with an erection from seeing me nude or nearly nude as he treated my sores from insect bites."

Lavon handed it back to her.

"Honey to be honest, I'd rather take you to bed but again you are too young. But I have already decided that if he wants me he can have me. He's certainly not the ugliest man I have ever slept with and to be once more honest, I could use a man right now. But let's wait and see what happens. He might not want me for a night, and he might not want me to tag along. Why don't we let nature take its course and not rush things? And where did you get a condom?"

"There were two boxes of them at the farm we stayed at. I packed them along with the first aid and toilet items before we left."

"Does Kevin know you have them?"

"He knew they were in the bathroom, but I have no idea if he knows I packed them."

"Why did you pack them Amanda?"

Amanda just looked at her with a neutral expression. Lavon just nodded her head and they both changed the subject while waiting for Kevin to finish with his bath. As Amanda, with Lavon's help, prepared the evening meal, Kevin set up the tent then hung a hammock between two trees at the top of the creek bank then a light tarp over that. It had only been a couple hours since Lavon ate but she ate a portion of the stew that Amanda had heated up and once dinner was over, Kevin went up the hammock and crawled inside of it without speaking. Amanda showed Lavon how they cleaned the dishes and then walked up to see Kevin.

"Kevin, are you sleeping up here tonight?"

"Yeah kiddo, you can share the tent with Lavon tonight, so you will not be alone."

"Kevin I'd rather sleep with you."

"I know you would but that's as good as it is going to get Amanda."

"Well wouldn't you rather sleep with Lavon then?"

"Amanda, drop it. I do not want this conversation between us."

Amanda moved and gave him a quick kiss on the lips before leaving him to his thoughts. She took a quick look around the camp then tossed both sleeping bags into tent and told Lavon to take either one tonight. Neither female spoke as they laid down and went to sleep. The next morning, they were awakened by the sound of metal as Kevin was getting ready to start a pot of coffee. Lavon exited with her pants in her hand and put them on as Kevin watched her in the dim light of the predawn morning. Since she was not wearing panties, Kevin got a fair view of her pubis before she covered it up with the sweat pants.

"Lavon…"

"Sorry Kevin, won't happen again. That tent is kind of small to be getting dressed in."

"Thank you, but what I was going to say was never go to bed without your sidearm as long as you are with us. Bad news can come from any direction during the night."

"Oh. Alright Kevin."

"After breakfast, gather your weapons and bags. We'll lay out a tarp and go through everything and refit you with what you need to continue on to Santa Fe."

"Certainly, Sergeant Barnes. Any other orders for the day?"

Kevin looked at her for a moment then stood and walked away. Lavon knew she had stepped over a line, but he had pissed her off. Why had he pissed her off was the one thing that was bothering her. She was not part of this tiny family, she was an intruder into it. Kevin climbed the creek bank and went out to check on the horses. None had lost their hobbles and were all within easy reach if needed. Seeing Lavon standing in the faint light had got to him and he knew that maybe his tone of voice was a bit harsh. He didn't know this woman and she didn't know him, but regardless she was causing him to rethink his celibacy and certainly not ending it with Amanda. He hated the fact he was only human in that aspect and she was certainly a woman. He was also aware that Amanda was putting herself in positions to be taken and used as a woman. Kevin could not figure out why she would be doing this after he had told her no so many times before.

Lavon found Kevin standing out in the pasture just looking back towards the horizon from where they had come from. When she spoke to him she startled him as he was deep in thought.

"Kevin, Amanda says come and eat before it gets cold."

Kevin turned to see Lavon standing slightly to his side behind him. She had changed her clothes and was now standing in her digital trousers and a t-shirt with her M4 slung over her right shoulder ready to use.

"Lavon, why are you here?"

"Amanda sent me to get you. Why?"

"No Lavon, why are you here now, in this place with us?"

"I have no idea what you mean, but I'm here until you tell me to leave."

Kevin looked at her for a moment before walking past her towards the creek and breakfast. After breakfast, he crossed the creek and walked until he was clear of the trees, searching the western skyline for signs of life such as smoke from a camp fire. He was almost half way back to camp when he heard a single gunshot from that direction. He knew it came from Lavon's M4 but not why which scared him. He ran through the woods and thick brush until he came to the edge of the creek bank. Looking across the creek he saw Lavon and Amanda sitting by the small campfire talking. He crossed the creek and walked up to them.

"What was that shot?"

Amanda pointed down the creek towards where they had their latrine set up and it took him a second to see the coyote lying in the brush. Then she spoke.

"I was using the latrine when the coyote came up and was snarling at me. Lavon shot it before I could even think to go for my pistol."

Kevin walked to the coyote and saw it was mangy and had a bullet hole in its head. He looked back towards the camp and depending on where Lavon was when she fired, it was roughly fifty yards through brush. Kevin reached into his trousers leg pouch for a length of parachute cord he always carried, carefully tied it to the coyote's rear legs and drug it down the creek for almost three hundred yards before just walking away. When he arrived back at the camp, the girls had laid out a tarp and had all of Lavon's gear spread out on it and was going through it to set up a single pack. He watched for several minutes before speaking.

"Lavon, I would like for you to take Amanda with you to Santa Fe. She should be safe there with you."

"No Kevin. I won't go."

"Amanda, please. Where I am going it is going to be risky as it is. I'm not sure I can take care of you."

"No Kevin. I won't go and there is nothing you can do to make me go with Lavon. Can Lavon go with us and help you take care of me?"

Kevin looked at Lavon who had a surprised looked on her face. She was looking back and forth between the two of them waiting to see who would win this argument. Lavon finally asked a question of Kevin.

"Kevin, where are you actually heading?"

"My Uncle's place just southwest of Breckenridge. Why?"

"Denver is due south from Cheyenne then on to Colorado Springs. That entire area was a battle field from the last communication we received from the Marine Reserve unit in Denver. That is one reason I'm in Kansas instead of Colorado or even Northern New Mexico by now. That's been weeks ago but do you think your uncle is still alive?"

Kevin thought about what she said then went to his saddlebags and retrieved the maps of Colorado. His uncle's place would be right on the western edge of what Lavon had talked about. His first thought was if Lavon was telling the truth or lying to get him to take her along with them. Or get him to change directions and head for Santa Fe. If she was telling the truth, then was all he had done so far been a waste of time? He looked back at the two of them sitting on the tarp watching him and decided no, it had not been a waste of time. He had saved Amanda which by itself was worth every ounce of effort he had expended.

He looked at Amanda and remembered how she looked the first time he laid eyes on her. Now she looked like a normal girl of her age and in fact had seemed to blossom out a bit more. Kevin suddenly felt very tired. He put the maps back into his saddlebag and just sat down next to the waning campfire and stared into it. Suddenly Lavon's boots were in his vision and he looked up at her.

"Kevin, we've got this. Go into the tent and get some rest. Amanda says you have hardly slept since she has been with you, waking up at the slightest noise. We'll watch while you sleep and wake you for dinner. Go, get some sleep."

It suddenly dawned on him that besides being a woman, Lavon was a Marine. He had some contact with Women Marines in Afghanistan and knew they were a force of their own when pressed. Kevin never spoke to either of them as he stood then walked to the tent, dropped his gear, unzipped the door and stepped inside with pistol in hand leaving the door partially open. As he lay down, for the first time since his Father's death, Kevin went to sleep feeling he was safe. He was asleep in minutes of removing his boots and clothing.

Lavon turned back to Amanda and just shrugged her shoulders before going back to sort through the uniforms and equipment. Amanda asked Lavon to teach how to use the M4 Carbine and they spent over an hour going through the function and how to hold it adjusting the stock to fit Amanda. Lavon had the ballistic vest from the man she had left Cheyenne with and fitted it to Amanda, so she would now have some protection.

When Kevin woke his body ached and his throat was parched. It took him a minute to get his bearings as he slowly sits up realizing he had a stiff neck and a headache. It was dark, and he found his jacket, removed the penlight from it and looked at his watch. It was 0437 meaning if it was dark then it was morning. He wasn't certain the time he had laid down, but he figured he must have slept at least fifteen hours. Kevin got his pants and boots on then opened the tent door enough to step out into the fresh air.

Lavon was sitting near the fire, wrapped in her poncho liner watching him as he stretched. She reached for the coffee pot at the edge of the small fire and poured a cup of coffee, then offered it to him as he looked at her. He walked to her, took the cup and thanked her. The coffee was very warm but not too hot to drink as he stood looking at the tarp which had been strung for cover and Amanda asleep under it.

"We've been doing two on two off, so you could sleep. I'm supposed to get her up at five but since you are up now, I think I'll just let her sleep a while longer. So, how are you feeling this chilly morning?"

Kevin had not even felt the chill until she commented about it. He took another long sip of the coffee and looked down at her.

"Did I eat dinner last night?"

"No, Amanda tried to wake you up, but you were sleeping the sleep of the dead. Kevin, she was very concerned about you."

"She is a good kid. Listen, Lavon go get a couple hours, I'll wake both of you up at seven then we can start planning our next move from here."

"Our next move?"

"Yes, our next move. I'd like you to stay with us unless you have a better offer."

"No better offer and no specific place to be at the moment, so I'll accept your offer."

She stood leaving the poncho liner on the ground as she stood, stepped to him, pulled his head down and kissed him.

"I'm not going to jump in bed with you to pay for my rations, but once we get to know each other better, plan on going to sleep with a smile on your face."

"You may not like me once you get to know me. But I make no demands on you other than help me protect Amanda. It's the only good thing I have done since this started."

Lavon gave him a quick peek on the lips then gathered up her poncho liner.

"Kevin, you are a good man, better than you think. Another other man would have taken Amanda since she had offered herself, but you haven't. I'll see you at seven."

She turned and waked over to the where Amanda was sleeping, took her boots off and made sure her weapons were within reach before rolling up in her poncho liner and using her shoulder bag as a pillow went to sleep. Kevin finished getting dressed, added a couple small pieces of wood to the fire and decided he needed to take a piss. He just walked to the creek and emptied his bladder before moving up to the top of the creek bank to looked towards the east. Far to the northeast was a red glow. Somewhere just over the horizon there was a fire. A large fire probably a farm house on fire. Nature caused, or purpose set was the question in his mind.

* * * * * * * * *

Journal Entry, June 7th.

I think karma hates me. Out of nowhere Marine Corporal Lavon Kincaid entered our camp. She is an attractive, black female about my age, maybe a year or so younger. I had decided to send Amanda with her as she was going to Santa Fe, so I could go alone to Colorado, but Lavon had information about the area where Uncle Henry's place is located, and I've changed my plans about Colorado. We're all going to Santa Fe.

I have not had a good night's sleep since Dad was killed but with Lavon here, being a Marine, I finally had a night's sleep. But when I got up, Lavon planted a kiss on me that almost seemed as if she was about to rip my clothes off and she told me to be prepared for just that later. I don't understand women. We barely know each other yet I have to say I could use some of that to help take my mind off Amanda always being so near.

* * * * * * * * *

Once the females were up and about they spent the day reorganizing the packs, distributing items so Lavon would have a horse to ride. She had ridden before, so Kevin was not too worried about her. Looking at the things she had brought into camp he asked her why she had brought her friends pack which had to be an extra burden on her.

"Well, David was not much bigger than me, so I could wear his uniforms although his t-shirts and such won't fit well over my breasts. But they will fit Amanda nicely, so she now has some extra clothing to wear. I was certainly not going to leave his ammunition and what was left of his rations behind. So, I just packed his stuff leaving out those personal things of his and drug it along."

The one item Kevin was glad to see was the night vision goggles. Lavon said the batteries were dead, but Kevin just smiled since he had a nice supply of rechargeable batteries they could use in them. Ever since leaving his parent's farm, Kevin had draped the roll-up solar panel over one of the pack horses and let batteries recharge as they moved during the daylight. They obtained a small, fold up solar panel at the farm he and Amanda had stayed at and often set it up when needed.

For three more days, they stayed at this location getting ready to make their next move. At night, they kept a two on, four off watch rotation. Amanda admitted it scared her to be up by herself at night but knowing they were close and she had her weapons made her less nervous. Kevin took the AR-15 he had been packing around and swapped the semi-automatic lower with the full automatic from the extra one Lavon had and then took Amanda down the creek for over a mile and taught her how to shoot it. He didn't want her to have a full automatic weapon until she was more experienced with it.

The extra Beretta was a bit large for Amanda's hands, so she just put her Ruger Mark II where the Beretta normally was carried on the vest along with her magazines. She liked the idea of having the body armor but did comment that she was glad she was not walking because of the weight. They cleaned out the extra camel back with mouthwash they had taken from the last farm and fitted it to Amanda, so she would have a good supply of water during the day.

Everything was packed other than what they needed for the evening and morning. Clothes had been washed, dried and packed. After an early dinner, Kevin had the females bathe before he took his turn as he gathered the horses up and brought them closer to the camp. When it was his turn he waited until they were out of sight on top of the creek bank. He kept his back to the camp as he cleaned himself and when he turned around to step out and dry himself, Lavon was lying on a saddle blanket in all her glory. She smiled at him and wiggled a finger indicating he was to join her. Other than the kisses they shared that morning before she laid down, they had barely touched except within the movements around the camp performing the tasks required.

Kevin looked around for Amanda but could not see her as he moved to the saddle blanket. He smiled at Lavon and joined her on the blanket. They wasted no time other than insuring both were ready for the act of coupling. She wanted him hard and fast and he wanted to take his time but once things got hot, he gave her what she asked for. Kevin was surprised he lasted as long as he did considering how long it had been since he had any manner of sex.

They were laying on the blanket with her head on his shoulder and leg across his when Amanda spoke.

"So, do you adults feel better now?"

Kevin tried to cover himself up with his hands as Lavon laughed at the situation. She raised up and looked at Amanda.

"Hell, yes Amanda, I know I feel a whole lot better now and if Kevin doesn't than we might have to do this again, so he does."

Amanda laughed then walked over to the tent, unzipped the door and looked back at them.

"I have the first watch, so why don't the two of you move into the tent and get some rest. Lavon, I'll get you up to relieve me."

Amanda moved to where her back was to them as they got up, gathered their clothing and other things and moved to the tent. Lavon never tried to be quiet as they had sex a second time about thirty minutes later. When Amanda woke Lavon up, Lavon was draped across Kevin. After Lavon had dressed and was ready to take over the watch, she gave Amanda a soft kiss on her lips.

"Thank you, Amanda. Now go get some sleep."

Amanda went to her sleep pad and within minutes was sound asleep. When Lavon woke Kevin for his watch they kissed long and hard before she walked over to where she had been sleeping next to Amanda, and laid down pulling Amanda next to her and insuring they were both covered from the night air. Kevin could only smile at the situation he had found himself in.

* * * * * * * * *

Journal Entry, June 11th.

Lavon gave herself to me yesterday and I have to think it was with Amanda's approval since she later seemed happy that I had sex with Lavon, even suggesting we sleep together in the tent. So, it looks like there is a fringe benefit to having Lavon along besides helping take care of Amanda.

* * * * * * * * *

When they left just after sunrise, Kevin rode out about a mile ahead of the girls with Amanda leading the pack horses and Lavon riding trail watching behind them plus ready to move forward if Kevin needed her. Kevin and Amanda had been using civilian FRC radios to communicate when they were far enough apart that yelling was not practical. Lavon had Motorola radios with rechargeable batteries and she kept in contact with Kevin using them.

June 21st

Another Refuge

They crossed into Colorado turning south-southwest figuring on cutting through the very tip of the Oklahoma Panhandle before entering New Mexico. They were having to cross larger creeks and rivers at bridges which concerned both Kevin and Lavon. The routine for crossing them became set piece with Kevin crossing usually on foot insuring it was safe then Lavon and Amanda bringing the horses across once he was certain it was safe to cross. This slowed the travel time down, but it was certainly safer than just moving on as if it was a Sunday ride out in the fresh air.

The weather had turned cooler and they endured days of rain as they moved on. This far out into the High Plains they were alone as they saw signs of early travelers leaving trash and the remains of bodies from time to time along the more traveled roads as they prepared to cross a river but no signs of recent travel ahead of them. When the weather was such that the three of them shared the tiny tent, Kevin and Lavon restrained themselves of any sexual contact because of Amanda being there with them.

Kevin had cut poles to use to erect a cover to protect them outside the tent from the rain, but cooking had to be done on either the Sterno stoves or a single burner propane stove using one-pound bottles. Slowly the supply of propane was dwindling as was the Sterno, but the value of a hot meal and drink was too important not to use it even sparingly. No one talked about how miserable they were as they moved on getting fifteen to twenty miles a day on a good day.

Amanda became a bit sullen even though she tried to keep a good face on the situation. Neither Kevin nor Lavon approached her about the situation other than to try to keep a good face on the conditions they were experiencing. Kevin had been keeping a small journal since he left his family farm and Amanda asked what month and day it was after evening chow. When Kevin asked her why after he told her the date, she just sat and quietly told them that her birthday was next week.

Kevin and Lavon were standing on a rise looking down at a farm that appeared to be abandoned. They had been traveling for eleven days and the rain had stopped the day before but at nearly five thousand feet above sea level the early morning air was chilled. They watched the farm for over an hour looking for any signs of life but the high grass around the house told them no one had been walking around and there was no path between the house and barn as if people had been walking there.

There were two cars in front of the house and a one-ton pickup behind the house hooked to a horse trailer. Kevin laid out the manner in which they were going down to the farm and then set off ahead of the others. He was in the lead with Lavon behind him then Amanda bringing up the rear with the pack horses. They gathered at the rear of the barn then he slowly went through the barn looking for anyone or anything which might be a danger to them. The stalls were open and empty which slightly bothered him since even if empty, he was taught to keep the stall gates closed.

Kevin exited the barn heading for the house with Lavon standing just inside the barn door covering him. Amanda was still mounted and ready to take the pack horses away from the farm if shooting started. Lavon followed about thirty feet behind Kevin and took cover behind the horse trailer as he moved on to the house. He was almost to the rear patio when Lavon called out to him to return to the horse trailer. Kevin kneeled and looked at the house for a long time before backing up then turning towards Lavon seeing that she had him covered from the trailer.

At the trailer, she pointed to the slats in the side of the trailer and when Kevin looked in he saw why the farm was abandoned. Inside the trailer was the remains of four decomposed bodies. Kevin opened the doors to the trailer and looked at them for a moment then closed the doors. From what he could see they all had their hands tied behind their backs and it appeared they had been shot in the back of the head. Any stench of decomposing had been washed away by the rains and time. Kevin looked at Lavon and then returned to the house.

The house looked as if the people who lived there had just left it with nothing appearing to have been disturbed. No dishes needing washed or food left out on the table. There was a musty smell which came from a house being closed over a period of time, but other than that, nothing to show why the bodies were in the trailer. Kevin found the basement door closed and carefully moved down the steps using a flashlight to see what was in front of him. In the basement, he had a minor fright as this light played on hanging plastic sheeting which reflected his light in an eerier manner.

In the basement were rolls of tables with planting pots on them and grow lights hanging above them. It looked as if the plants had been roughly removed from the mess of overturned pots and potting soil on the floor and tables. Kevin picked up a dried leaf from the floor and knew what had been growing there and probably why the bodies were in the trailer. This farmer had been growing marijuana in his basement. Colorado had legalized marijuana but was this a legal grow or a bootleg operation? As he turned to exit the basement he noticed the electrical fuse panel for the house was slightly open and looked inside to see the mains had been turned off.

Kevin tried the stove in the kitchen to see if it would fire off, but nothing happened. Outside of the house he found the propane tank and saw it had been turned off at the tank. He moved back to Lavon and told her what he had discovered before they went back to the barn and helped Amanda bring the horses in. There was plenty of hay and grain to feed the horses and the cattle tank outside the barn was nearly full from the rain. Once that was accomplished they took their personal bags into the house and opened it up to let fresh air in and clear the musky smell from it.

Amanda explored the bed rooms as Lavon checked out the master bedroom while Kevin returned to the propane tank and turned it on after insuring the hot water tank and other appliances using propane was turned off. While he was lighting the pilot lights to the cook stove Amanda brought in a notebook she had found in what was the daughter's room of the farmer. It was her English homework dated two days before the attack on the country. The picture of what had happened at the farm became clearer for Kevin. These people were killed for the marijuana and the house had been shut down to prevent an accidental fire from alerting authorities to the murders. Whoever had done this had been very professional in their actions.

Kevin went to the implement shed and found a trash pump used to transfer water from one place to another and found the gasoline motor would run. He moved it, so the intake was in the cattle tank and after two hours of searching and work had it hooked into the line from the well to the house. Once he had as low a pressure as possible into the house he lite the propane hot water tank and two hours later he and Lavon showered together in the master bath room after Amanda had taken her shower. They had all agreed that since this farm had been neglected for all these weeks and as isolated as it was, they could rest here for a few days and not worry about being bothered. Kevin told Amanda about the bodies in the trailer and said he would deal with them the next day.

Once Kevin had removed the bodies and buried them in a common, shallow grave, he set about looking for anything they could use during their trip. The girls went through the house looking in every closet and drawer and had moved furniture out of the way in the living room to make room for their baggage and the things they found. When Kevin came in for the evening meal after tending to the horses, he found both girls in dresses as they

66

prepared dinner from the canned foods in the house. Lavon's dress was at least a two-sizes too big for her, but they had pinned it so if would fit her better. Amanda's dress fit her well except it was cut for a girl with larger breasts which Amanda joke it was stuffed with hand towels to fill it out better. She did raise her skirt to show she was wearing actual girl panties and that they fit her well enough, so she would not have to keep wearing the boy briefs she had been wearing.

* * * * * * * * *

Journal Entry, June 21st.

We found an intact farm today along with the bodies of the family that lived here. They were killed, execution style. It looks like the farmer was growing marijuana in his basement and that was why the family was murdered.

This farm is so far off the beaten track we should be able to rest here and restock our supplies since we found a full pantry and it looks like the farmer was a bit of a prepper or survivalist considering all the freeze-dried food we have so far located.

Now I need to get the heavy-duty commercial generator running and we'll be in hog heaven for a time.

* * * * * * * * *

Kevin worked for two days to get a generator running and it took that long because he had to charge the twelve-volt battery it required with the solar panels. Once it was up and running he hooked it into the water well and reconnected the well to the house. He ran an extension cord into the house to power the fans and move air around. There was plenty of gasoline in the storage tank to keep the generator was fueled, so they left it running only shutting it off to refuel and service.

Lavon turned out to be an excellent cook and using powered eggs and powered milk from Kevin's original food stock baked Amanda a birthday cake. Earlier in the day Amanda had been messing around with the television plugging it in to an extension cord and it came on. She plugged in the DVD/Blu-ray player and that worked. Amanda looked through the selection and picked out Johnny Depp's Alice in Wonderland and put it in. When the music started at the first of the movie Lavon came in to see what has happening. They let it play as they went about the chores that needed accomplished then that evening the three of them watched Nicolas Cage in the Sorcerer's Apprentice as they ate Amanda's cake.

After the movie, Amanda hopped up on Kevin's lap, gave him a big kiss then leaned over and gave Lavon a quick peek, hopped off and announced she was going to bed and for them not to make too much noise tonight. Kevin had a shocked look on his face as Lavon laughed at the situation. When they went to bed, Kevin immediately noticed that Lavon had completely shaved her body while he had been out tending to the horses and generator. She had not shaved her legs or elsewhere once leaving Cheyenne which did not bother him considering the circumstances.

The days were taken up with reorganizing the packs, sorting and insuring the food packs were protected plus making up packets such as oatmeal broken down into three-person servings in zip lock bags. Sugar, salt, coffee and other condiments were broken down as needed and carefully packed. Lavon found a cast iron cook book and experimented with making bread using a biscuit recipe and made up packets for making a single pot of bread using powdered milk and powdered eggs from Kevin's stash saving the fresher ingredients found in the house for packaging. Nothing glass went into the packs and plastic jars were wrapped with duct tape to prevent the lids from popping off in the bags.

The fifth wheel camper parked next to the implement shed was gone through for anything that might be useful including two additional sleeping bags if needed to protect from the cold as they moved into a higher climate.

June 27th

Unwanted Visitors

They had spent nearly a week at this farm and were considering when to move on when as Kevin was at the barn tending to the horses just before dinner he looked out to the ridge where they had come from and saw horsemen. He was carrying an eight-power monocular in his vest and took a good look to ensure that he was seeing riders and not just horses. Kevin keyed his radio.

"Lavon, we have four riders on the ridge to the east. Get ready and get Amanda ready."

Lavon responded and pulled her digital uniform jacket over her t-shirt and jeans then pulled her vest on as she was giving Amanda instructions. Amanda went into over drive getting her camouflage shirt on and then her vest. They met in the kitchen as Kevin announced the riders have left the ridge heading their way. Lavon told Amanda to stay on the enclosed back porch and do not hesitate to shoot if necessary. Lavon headed to the barn as fast as possible and told Kevin she was headed up into the loft.

Kevin watched as Lavon climbed the ladder, blew him a kiss from the loft then disappeared into the darkness of the loft. He watched the riders as they closed the gap to the barn and stepped out, so they would have to come to him and not the house. What he did not know was that Amanda had moved from the porch and was kneeling at the rear of the pontoon boat where she could see past the corner of the barn and the men that was approaching it. Amanda was scared but knew that both Kevin and Lavon were depending on her if things got nasty. She looked down at the selector switch on the rifle and moved it to fire. The training they had been giving her kicked in and she kept her finger off the trigger now that it was ready to fire since she had chambered a round before leaving the porch.

As the men approached, Kevin took one last look with his monocular identifying the weapons they were carrying. From left to right the riders were carrying a lever action rifle, a shotgun, an AR-15, and another lever action rifle. Lavon whispered in his ear that the AR was probably the leader. She was right.

The riders spread out as they approached Kevin and the barn. Lavon was positioned back in the shadows and could see the two men to the leader's right, Kevin's left, but she could not see the man to Kevin's right. Amanda had a clear vision of the man on the far right but only a partial view of the man in front of Kevin and no view of the others. She was praying they were peaceful and that Lavon had the other men covered. Kevin opened the conversation as polite as possible.

"Can I help you gentlemen?"

"Yeah, drop the shotgun mister. We're deputies trailing some folks that are raiding and killing innocent people for whatever they can steal."

Kevin never shifted the shotgun which was hanging in front of him as he would have carried his AK or M4. The men were filthy and wore no badges of office.

"Deputies, well I don't see any badges and sorry, the shotgun stays right where it is for now."

"Dude, put the shotgun down and call your women out so we can take them into custody." One of the men to his left spoke. Kevin never took his eyes off the leader.

"Women, what women?" He replied.

"We know you have two women with you. Bring them out so we can take a look at them." The other man spoke again. The look on the leader's face was not one Kevin appreciated.

"Gentlemen, why don't you ride on out of here before you find that you have made a major mistake."

Amanda had her rifle up and was looking at her man through the ACOG sight hoping that Kevin would make the men leave but when she saw the man stand up in his saddle and raise his rifle up to shoot at Kevin she never considered anything but the sight picture and trigger squeeze.

Kevin saw the man rising in his saddle in his peripheral vision then heard a single shot from around the barn and the man in the saddle jerk. The other men looked to their left at the man Amanda had shot, giving Kevin a second to react before they could. Lavon heard Amanda's shot and as she stepped out of the shadows, she clicked her M4 to full auto and took the far-left man with a four-round burst in the chest at the same time she heard Kevin's shotgun fire.

Amanda had fired hitting her target in the left side about half way down in the ribs with the bullet traveling through his left lung, ripping through his heart and then his right lung before exiting out the rib cage under the man's right arm pit. He was toppling off his horse when it spooked and bolted away from the noise of gunfire. The man's foot hung in a stirrup and was being dragged as the horse ran from the fight.

Kevin brought his shotgun up in one fluid motion and as the leader was turning his head back to look at him, Kevin fired center mass. At the distance between the two of them, all nine 00 buckshot pellets impacted in his chest. As he turned on the man to his left and he fired, he heard a second group of automatic fire from the loft and as his pellets were hitting his second target, Lavon's bullets were also ripping through the man. It was over in seconds.

Lavon stepped to the edge of the loft door and looked down at Kevin who was standing, looking at the scene before him.

"Kevin!" They both heard Amanda yelling as she came running around the barn. As soon as she saw Kevin standing with the bodies in front of him she stopped and just starred. Kevin looked at Amanda as she looked at him then she looked down at her rifle and flipped the selector to safe and lowered the muzzle to the ground. Kevin moved to her as she stood there looking down at the ground. He took her in his arms as she began to shake. He just held her as she began to cry.

"It's alright Amanda. Everything is going to be alright now."

"Kevin, that man was going to shoot you. I had no choice, I had to shoot him."

"I know kiddo, I know. Thanks for taking care of me Honey." He kissed her on top of her head as he saw Lavon come trotting up to them. She took a quick look at the two of them then moved to check to insure the men were dead. When she walked back to Kevin she had the leader's AR-15 in her right hand and the magazine from it in her left hand. She handed the magazine to Kevin who took it with his free hand and immediately noticed it was light, meaning even though it was a thirty-round magazine it was probably less than a third full. Looking into the magazine he saw the ammunition was soft pointed ammunition, hunting ammunition instead of full metal jacket such as Lavon and Amanda had in their magazines.

"Lavon, please take Amanda back into the house while I deal with this mess."

Lavon gently peeled Amanda away from Kevin and wrapped an arm around her shoulder as she guided her back to the farm house. Kevin looked at the bodies determining if he was going to waste his time burying them or just leaving them to the elements. Two of the horses had come back to their riders, a third was about fifty yards away just standing, while the fourth, the one that had drug his rider was a couple hundred yards away grazing.

Kevin first gathered up the weapons noticing they all had rust on them, insured they were safe as he emptied each one. None of the weapons were fully loaded to capacity. Next came the bodies as he emptied each pocket and removed any pistols and knives before tying their feet together and spinning the bodies all facing the same direction. The horses that were nearby, he gathered up and tied their reins to the corral fence before he tied a rope to the feet of the men, then using the leader's horse, drug the bodies to the forth man, searched and stripped him of weapons and items before adding him to the group.

He dragged the bodies back over the rise and just let the rope drop, leaving the bodies to the elements. Kevin looked back to the farm and thought about what the one man had said about having two women with him and wondered how long they had watched the farm before moving down to it. Both Amanda and Lavon's hair had grown out long and had they mistaken Amanda for being a woman instead of a girl? Then he considered that Amanda's age would not have mattered to them as they would have used her as they would have used Lavon if they could have gotten their hands on them. As he rode back to the farm and gathered up the last horse, he smiled to himself that they might have gotten their hands-on Lavon, but it would not have been easy and certainly not after a fight.

Kevin unsaddled the horses, took their bridles and harnesses off and released them to the wild. There was plenty of grass and the pond to the south was full. He put the saddles in the barn then carried their saddle bags and other bags to the back porch and dropped them to go through later. He went to the sink and washed his hands and forearms before turning to look at the AR-15 that was lying on the table. Lavon had broken it down and it was a mess. Rust and carbon build-up on the bolt carrier group and

Kevin wondered if it would have even cycled even if it did fire. He was thinking that even professional criminals would know to keep the tools of their trade clean and ready to use.

Lavon came back into the kitchen, pulled herself tight to him and kissed him with a passion he had yet to feel from her even with some of the action they had shared in bed. When she broke the kiss she just held onto him and he could feel a slight tremor from her body.

"Lavon, are you okay?"

"Yeah, I'm alright, but I was scared to death up till the shooting started then nothing. I just reacted to the situation."

"Honey, you were trained well. How is Amanda?"

"She was shaking so badly by the time we got to the house I gave her a pain pill to calm her down. I have some Hydrocodone from when I pulled a muscle in my shoulder a few months ago. It hit her almost immediately and I put her to bed. Part of her is scared that you will be mad at her for not staying on the porch."

Kevin gently eased away from Lavon and picked up the Bolt Carrier Group lying on the table.

"I'm glad she didn't because the man she killed was already up in the saddle before I recognized the threat. I was expecting the owner of this piece of crap to take the first shot. Stupid bastards letting their weapons get in such bad shape."

"Kevin, how did that other man know there were two women here? I mean, if they were close enough to see us, then they had to be closer than we think?"

"Honey, I've given that some thought and the only thing I could come up with was at least one of them was watching us with binoculars while waiting for the others to catch up. Only thing that makes sense. Your hair is longer than regulation and Amanda's is very long. Both of you have been outside today so they saw the

74

long hair and put two and two together and came up with that answer. I guess that only seeing me they figured they had us out numbered and out gunned. They never figured on facing a female Marine."

"Or the fact we females knew how to defend ourselves. But that was too close Kevin. If Amanda had not left the patio and taken the shot, your vest might have kept you from being killed but we'd be treating your wounds by now. Kevin, you do know she is in love with you, don't you?"

"Lavon, I'm not very good with female emotions. I once thought a girl was in love with me, but I was wrong. She gave me her virginity as she took mine and for two years we had sex whenever we could find a private place. But she left me for an older man and the last time I saw her she had a kid in hand and one in the oven. I've had other lovers, but they were just passing the time with me, so I never took any of it serious other than do the best I could in bed."

"Well lover you do very well in bed and if Amanda was at least fifteen, I'd tell you go make her happy."

"Lavon, fifteen is still too young.   At least it is for me. Maybe I'm old fashioned in this but it is how I am. Can we please change the subject?"

"Sure Kevin, I'm sorry, and I will never bring it up again. Now, I wonder why those men came after us when they did."

"They saw me away from the house and I guess they figured I would be an easy target instead of trying to take me in the house. They were all short of ammunition which meant they could not keep up a firefight for more than a minute or two.   Granted, they probably didn't know how we were armed but digging us out of the house would be difficult.   Which makes me wonder why they didn't wait until later when we might be asleep or ambush me in the morning as I left the house. I haven't looked through their bags yet, but something tells me they were probably hungrier than horny."

"Kevin, how much longer are we going to stay here?"

Kevin looked around the kitchen and just gave a sigh.

"I think we need to leave within the next forty-eight hours. Maybe sooner. Let's see how Amanda is doing when she wakes up."

"I'm already awake." Amanda spoke from the door.

Kevin stepped away from Lavon as she turned towards the door to look at Amanda.

"Kevin, please take me where I never have to pick up or use a gun again. Please."

It was almost a cry as she spoke. Kevin went to her and took her in his arms and held her tight.

"I'm sorry Amanda that you had to do what you did. You most likely saved my life and I shall always be grateful." He kissed her on top of her head.

"When you first taught me to shoot, I never actually considered killing another person. I just wanted to please you anyway I could and to take some of the worry I knew you had for me off your mind. I was scared out there and to be honest I never thought when I shot that man other than he was about to shoot you. It wasn't until it was all over that I realized what I had done."

"Amanda, I'll let you in on a secret. I was also scared as I was waiting for the shooting to start. I was afraid that I would be killed and there would be no one to protect you and Lavon. Those were not the first men I ever killed but they deserved to die for what they intended to do to you and Lavon. Honey, I don't have any other words that might make this easier for you, but I thank you with all my heart for what you did today."

Amanda pushed away from Kevin and looked at him then Lavon before looking back at Kevin.

"Sleep with me tonight. I don't mean make love to me or even touch me, just sleep with me as we once did."

"Amanda, I'll sleep with you as we once did. After dinner and you shower, put on some pajamas and if you wish, you can sleep between me a Lavon tonight. Our bed is big enough for the three of us."

Amanda looked at Lavon who smiled at her and nodded her approval. She reached up and pulled Kevin down and gave him a quick kiss and then walked to Lavon and kissed her before moving to where she had tonight's dinner laid out and began the process of preparing dinner. Lavon looked at Kevin and winked before turning to help Amanda. Kevin just took a deep breath and picked up the pieces of the AR off the table and set them aside until after dinner.

The girls noticed Kevin seemed distracted more than usual at dinner. He was always seeming to think of what had to be done next and often talked to the girls about tomorrow's chores but tonight he seemed more distracted. Kevin did not seem upset about the events of the day, but it was as if he was trying to work out a problem that he could not find the answer too. Finally, Lavon asked him if there was something wrong.

"Lavon, we have been through every room in this house and I have yet to find a firearm or even a gun cabinet. A person growing marijuana had to have had at least one firearm in the house and I can understand who ever killed those people taking it. But this is the first farm I have ever been on that did not have someplace to store even the most basic of firearms."

"Did you look in the room in the basement?" Amanda asked.

"What room?" Kevin inquired.

"The one behind the plastic curtain on the right after you step off the stairs."

"I never looked behind the plastic. I figured there was only walls. Never considered there might be a door there. How did you find it?"

"I dropped a can of peas and it rolled under the plastic. I saw the door when I raised the plastic to get the can. I'm sorry I didn't say anything, but you are normally very thorough in looking for things."

"No problem Honey. I'll check it out while you shower and get ready for bed."

After they got the kitchen cleaned up for the evening, Kevin went down and started cutting the heavy plastic away from the wall. He found the door which he had to smile at since it had been painted to look like the cinderblocks that made up the basement wall. He had brought all the keys that he had found upstairs and went through them but could not find the key to the heavy steel door. He looked around the basement then went under the steps and found a single key hanging from a small nail.

Lavon came down as he was preparing to unlock the door and he paused for a moment. The door was hidden behind heavy plastic where it could not be clearly seen plus it was painted to look like the cinder blocks. Whatever is behind the door has value which Kevin thought if he was trying to hide the room he would also do something to protect its contents. He looked at Lavon and just motioned for her to get away front the front of the door and he moved to put the cinderblock between him and the room and reached over and gently opened the door a couple of inches.

He waited a full ten count, then moved to the door and using his flashlight scanned the partial opening looking for anything that might hint of danger. He was not sure, so he eased it open another inch then about the middle of the top of the door he

78

saw the monofilament line hanging between the door frame and the top of the door. He opened the door another inch as he watched the line slow tighten. Kevin reached up over the door and felt for what the line might be attached too and found something he recognized by touch. He closed his eyes and let his fingers examine how it was set into place and once he had it pictured in his mind, he took a deep breath, grasped the pin holding the device in a safe condition and pushed the door open, breaking the line. He lifted the device up from its holder and brought it down to look at. He pushed the pin completely back into the firing device of the M67 Fragmentation grenade and bent the pin over, so it would not accidently come out.

Kevin stepped away from the door and just held the grenade out to Lavon who stepped to take it from his hand. He moved back to the door and continued to examine the door and frame as he opened it. When he had the door open enough to move through it, he moved in and looked up at the can attached to the top of the door. The grenade rested with the arming lever on the outside of the can so when the line pulled the pin, the action of the arming lever flipping off would cause the grenade to fall through the open bottom and onto the floor as the four to five second fuse burned. Ingenious in nature and unless someone was looking for this booby trap, they would most likely die before they realized they had tripped it. And the way it was rigged, the owner only had to reach up and pull the grenade up and out of the can insuring the pin stayed in place as he had just done. Resetting the trap was just a reverse of the process.

He looked around the room as best he could with his flashlight and smiled before stepping out and closing the door. Kevin looked at Lavon as she just stood holding the grenade.

"Baby, in the morning we are going to run a couple of extension cords down here and put some light and a fan in there. We have hit a gold mine."

He walked over to her, took her face in his hands and kissed her.

"Let's get a shower and go to bed."

Lavon laughed. "Remember, we have company in bed tonight."

"I haven't forgotten, but there is a lot of room in that shower."

Amanda was sitting up in their bed when they entered the bedroom reading by the oil lamp on the nightstand. Lavon stripped for the shower while Kevin stopped at removing his boxer shorts. He picked up a clean pair from his bag and took them along with his pistol into the bathroom as Lavon proceeded him also carrying her pistol. Kevin looked over at the night stand next to Amanda to see her pistol there in case it was needed. They had already set the trips inside the house and after a long and sexual shower, they blew out the lamp and went to sleep with Amanda in the middle under separate covers from Kevin. When Kevin woke in the morning, Amanda had her head up on his shoulder, snuggled in next to him but still wrapped up in her own covers like a cocoon. He kissed her on the forehead and gently removed her from him, so he could get up and start the day.

* * * * * * * * *

Journal Entry, June 28.

Amanda killed a man yesterday that was trying to kill me. Four men rode up on horses demanding the women. Amanda killed the first man, then between Lavon and myself, we took care of the other three. Those men were stupid and incompetent as far as I'm concerned. Their weapons were filthy and starting to rust plus they were low on ammo.

I hurt inside because of what Amanda had to do to protect me and herself. I let her sleep with Lavon and myself last night. Regardless of her age, I do have strong feelings for Amanda. Feelings that I think are wrong to be having.

80

* * * * * * * * *

Kevin was sitting at the table drinking a cup of coffee when Lavon entered, gave him a kiss then went for her own cup of coffee. She sat down across from him and just smiled as she looked at him.

"Okay Lavon, what's on your mind?"

"I realized that the reason you have not touched Amanda is because you love her. Not the kind of love that lovers feel but more like brother and sister. She told me how the two of you came to be together and how you refused to take her at the beginning. You are an amazing man considering the situation and how screwed everything is right now."

"Lavon, the condition she was in and the situation we have found ourselves in is no excuse to violate a girl that young, even if she was willing to be violated. It's that simple as far as I am concerned. And yes, I suppose I do love her in a fashion. She has been a good companion and has helped a lot once she started eating better and regained a lot of strength. I would be lying if I said it wasn't a strain at first not to take her up on her offer."

"And if I hadn't come along, you'd still not have taken her by now?"

"Baby, I would like to think she would still be a virgin even once we departed or at least got to our final destination."

"So, what are your plans for today? Back to the basement?"

"Oh yes, once we get the lights and fan down there, we'll move everything into the living room and see what we have to deal with. But I'd like to get back on the road within a couple days if possible."

Lavon stood and started for towards the bedrooms before stopping and turning back.

"I'm getting Amanda up but Kevin, you have to tell her how you feel about her. Her hormones are raging, and she thinks all she has to give you for everything you have done is her body. Now she has killed a man to protect you. She has earned the right to know."

Kevin watched her leave the kitchen before taking another drink of coffee then gathering up his vest and AK before going out to service the generator before Breakfast. He was nervous being out in the pre-dawn morning knowing if someone was out there to cause him harm, he was on his own. He was also scared for the girls being trapped in the house even though Lavon would fight hard to protect Amanda if necessary. Yes, he loved Amanda like a little sister but had yet decided how he felt about Lavon. The passion between them was real but he had yet to determine what exactly was driving that passion.

Breakfast was canned Corned Beef Hash and powdered eggs with toast made from bread Lavon had baked the day before. After breakfast, he went to the implement shed and found enough additional extension cords to run from the generator to the basement and clip on lights for the room. He set a fan in the door to remove the musty smell and clipped a light to the top of the door to light the room before going back up to the kitchen for a cup of coffee as he waited for a few minutes before beginning the task of cleaning out the room.

Amanda had just finished with the morning dishes when Lavon gave him a short kiss, looked at Amanda and then left the room to leave them alone. Kevin asked Amanda to take a seat in front of him and he took her hands in his as he looked into her eyes, as he tried to find the words she needed to hear.

"Amanda, listen carefully please. I'm not very good with words especially when dealing females of any age. When we first met, and you offered yourself to me, the animal side of me, of any man did give some thought to enjoying what you had to offer. But you have to know that I was not raised that way and I have experiences that keeps telling me how wrong it is for a girl your age to be used in such a manner."

He paused for a moment.

"Remember me telling you about my trek from my apartment to my family farm? Well during that time, I killed two men that had just raped then murdered an old woman for no reason other than to rob her and use her for their own sick pleasure. What kind of man would I be to kill two men for doing what you were prepared for me to do to you? Do you understand what I am saying?"

"Yes Kevin, you would have been a hypocrite. You would have been no better than the men you killed. If I understand correctly."

"Yes, and I was not raised that way. Now when we met you were a mess. Eaten up with insect bites and undernourished. You are filling out to be a lovely young lady, one that in a few years will attract a lot of suitors wishing to enjoy your favors and your body. Amanda, I do love you, but I love you as a brother not as a man who would take you to his bed and make love to you. You owe me nothing more than what you have been doing by my side these few weeks we have been together and yesterday you did more than I could ever hope for in protecting me."

"Kevin, I never thought as I saw that man raising his rifle to shoot you. I just shot him and was praying you and Lavon could handle the rest of them. I was so scared Kevin."

"I know baby, I know. I was scared too but more scared for you and Lavon than myself. I had already made up my mind to kill them before they had a chance to get their hands on you and use you up. You just started the fight a second or two before I did. Once more, thank you for protecting me from that man."

"I didn't want to shoot him. I really didn't, and I hope I never have to do anything like that again. But you can depend on me to help when I have to."

"Thank you. Now we need to get to work so we can see what the basement room has to offer and then get ready to leave this place. While Lavon and I clean out the room I need you to stay up here and watch in case someone else shows up to cause us problems."

"I can do that Kevin and if you don't mind, I'm going to try to make a cake. I've been helping Lavon and want to try one by myself."

"Sure Amanda, just don't get too distracted while mixing things up."

Kevin leaned over and gave her a kiss on her forehead then a quick peek on her lips before standing and looking at Lavon standing in the doorway. He smiled at her and turned for the basement door, never looking back to see if she was following.

It took nearly two hours to clear out the room with Lavon stopping in the kitchen from time to time to check on Amanda's attempt to bake a cake and answer questions before returning to the task at hand. When finished, they took a break and sampled the cake which Amanda had baked. Both told Amanda she did great for her first effort and the scratch chocolate icing was rich. Kevin went out to tend to the horses as the girls began to break into the cases of survival food they had brought up from the basement.

On one side of the living room was stacks of food while on the other was weapons and ammunition. There were several rifle hard cases, larger than the normal ones found in sporting goods stores which had military markings. Once the cases were opened, they found they had another problem, one which gave them a long pause in considering how they were already loaded down.

One case contained a Barrett M107A1 .50 BMG Sniper Rifle and another a M110 SASS (Semi-Automatic Sniper Rifle) which was based on the AR-10 platform firing a 7.62 NATO cartridge.   In searching the ammunition cans the located two hundred rounds of ammunition for the big Barrett and five hundred rounds of Lake City National Match ammunition for the M110.

"Kevin, we can't transport these rifles without at least one maybe two more horses and we have our hands full now as we move. But we just can't leave them here for just anyone to find and use."

Kevin thought for a minute before smiling.

"Sure, we can leave them. But we won't leave them in the house. I'll clean out a couple of stalls, dig holes and bury the things we can't take with us then cover them up with the old straw to make it look like nothing is there but horse manure."

Lavon laughed.

"Alright, sounds like a plan. Shall we get them out of the way before we get into the rest of this mess?"

They went back into the basement, rearranged the tables that were there for the growing of marijuana and then laid out the rifles. Kevin thought about the M110 for a bit but decided to hold off until they had gone through the other cases and boxes before determining if he would take it along. He and Lavon talked about why this farmer had these weapons and equipment as they sorted through the boxes in the living room. The food suggested he was a prepper, a survivalist, but the weapons suggested more to it than they could determine. Nothing in the house suggested he was a member of some militia group or such. And the computer in the living room was completely inoperable to see if there was anything in the computer's history files to show them what this individual was thinking.

Lavon did tell Kevin that about six months before the event, there was a message to tighten up their Reserve Center's security because of several break-ins at some armories across the country. Weapons and equipment were being stolen without a trace. This was never announced to the public and kept under tight wraps with specific instructions on dealing with theft to prevent public knowledge. They had found no photos or documents within the house showing this farmer had any military experience, yet he seemed to have a solid working knowledge of outfitting for battle. Body armor, equipment vest, weapons and other items needed were all there and ready to use. Vests were complete and ready to use. The only thing needed done was filling the weapons magazines with ammunition.

The one thing Kevin decided on when he first saw it was an AR-15 Short Barreled Rifle (SBR) with a silencer on it. As much as he liked his AK, he determined that they should all carry the same ammunition and magazines. The hardest decision was what to keep and what to leave from the weapons he had gathered up during his trip from his apartment. He would keep his father's revolver but the one he picked up from the dead farmer that first week would stay behind. Kevin would leave his AK behind in favor of the SBR after he changed the lower to a full automatic version, plus he would take one of the M-4's that was in the stash as a backup.

The pistols were another thing. Amanda had problems with the size of the grip on the M-9 Beretta's they had but she was comfortable with Kevin's Sig P2022. But the farmer had four of the Sig P-250's which Amanda was also comfortable with and after they took her out to shoot two magazines of ammunition through one, Kevin retired his 2022 to his saddlebags and they all would carry the 250's which were chambered in .40 Smith & Wesson.

They spent most of the day insuring the equipment vests were properly outfitted and fitted before moving to the next phase.

There was more than enough ammunition for both the handguns and rifles, so they decided to leave the 9mm handguns behind along with the ammunition to lighten the load at least that much. Amanda would keep her Ruger's for hunting and Lavon would have the Henry AR-7 take-down survival rifle in .22 Long Rifle as Kevin would keep his .410 shotgun for hunting. Here they got lucky in that the farmer had over a thousand rounds of .22 Long Rifle ammunition and two hundred rounds of .410 ammunition in Number 6 shot.

Everything else went into the barn before they started on the food with one exception. In one ammunition can they found five more M67 Fragmentation grenades with electrical tape wrapped around the arming levers to prevent accidental ignition of the firing mechanism. There were pouches for the grenades which Kevin attached four to his equipment belt and Lavon attached two. The tape was taken off the grenades and alcohol was used to remove the residual tape adhesive before placement into the pouches. Even with Lavon's and Amanda's help it still took two days to dig, bury the extra gear and cover it up. Kevin had in his mind that maybe someday he could return for the weapons and ammunition.

Amanda was lucky in that the farmer's daughter was close to her own size except for having larger breasts but the sports bras worked just fine for her. She did mention that the boots she had gained from the first farm were feeling tight and this girl wore a half size larger than Amanda. Kevin had Amanda go through all the girl's civilian clothing and fine things she could wear once they found some sort of civilization. Lavon helped her select and pack these clothes in a separate duffle then Lavon went through the closets to find things she might wear even though the lady of the house wore clothing three sizes larger.

Everything military that could be used by someone else that was not being taken was put in the barn. Lavon had sealed everything she could with a Seal-A-Meal to protect it from water and rust before going to the barn.   Next came the food stores. First was the twelve cases of military issue MRE's. The way they had the packs for the horses configured, leaving them in the cases would make it difficult to pack and carry so they emptied each case and tossed the empties into the basement. Instead of outfitting their larger field packs, Lavon and Kevin were outfitting the smaller three-day patrol packs which were in the stash. Three complete MRE's went into each pack for emergency, then two went into the saddle bags, also for emergencies. There were large Number 10 size cans of dehydrated food stuffs from beef and chicken to corn and peas. These they sat aside for later as they went through the boxes of vacuum packed backpacker's food. These were packaged in two and four-person meals. Amanda was thrilled to find a cartoon of freeze dried ice cream which Kevin said she could have all for herself. She snacked on one pack as they worked, and she put four in her patrol pack and the rest in her personal pack.

It took two days to rearrange the packs for the horses and determine what to leave and what to take. Lavon experimented with the foods from the large cans and found a formula for making a stew from the dehydrated meats and vegetables which she then packed in heat sealable packets using the Seal-A-Meal they also found in the pantry. There were premixed bread mixes which she tried using the cast iron pots and found she could make a passable bread if they had enough time on the trail.

They figured the travel time between their location and Santa Fe and doubled it then developed a basic menu for food and found they had enough food for three meals a day using the packets Lavon constructed first then the camper's meals before ever having to dig into the MRE's. Every magazine pouch was filled with loaded magazines and additional ammunition was spread out amongst the horses to balance the loads.

They did have to add two horses to the pack trail mostly due to the amount of food they could not justify leaving behind.

They also added a six-person tent to replace the small tent so when the weather was bad, they could all get out of the weather. Also, there was a twelve-foot square pop-up canopy with a light brown top and additional side curtains they added which they could put up when there were no trees to rig a tarp. They were becoming overloaded in many ways and knew that the load times in the morning and off load times in the afternoons would reduce their travel time but after being so long on short rations they could not leave anything behind which meant the need for the additional horses.

Cold weather gear was also added since at this elevation, winter comes quicker even though they were about to turn and head south towards warmer weather. Two combat Medic bags were added, which Amanda and Lavon would carry. Amanda found the military First Aid manual and began reading it when not busy doing other things. She took the bags apart learning what each item was and intended usage. Amanda also wore her complete vest setup from the time she got out of bed until she got ready for bed in order to get use to the weight. Aspirin became a staple for her during the first couple of days to ease the aches of the load on her smaller body.

Lavon handed Kevin a phone book and map then told him they needed to see if they could raid the local Walmart for feminine products since they were running low between her and Amanda. Amanda just stood by and listened to the discussion without speaking as the adults planned how to accomplish this and hopefully get in and out without attracting attention. Kevin told Lavon to get two of the large field packs from the basement, empty them out and they could use them on the raid. He'd carry one and she would carry the other. The plan would be that once hers was full she would trade out with him to fill the other, so he could keep watch.

One final check to insure all the batteries were charge since they had kept the solar panels operating since they had set up house then checked their night vision goggles to insure they were in proper functioning order. The packs were in the barn ready for loading as the additional horses were in stalls along with their original horses. Kevin had been feeding them grain from the feed room fattening them up some for the journey.

The farmer had commercial Motorola radios which had headsets meaning they could retire the military and FRC radios and everyone would be on the same radio now. At daylight, they left the barn with Kevin a half mile in the lead with Lavon and Amanda leading four pack houses each.

One question that had been bothering Kevin, but he never took time to check out was the location of the horses and cattle that had to be part of this farm. That question was answered a mile later after they crossed a low water bridge through a stand of trees and he came upon a gate. On the other side of the gate were three horses and over twenty head of cattle in a large pasture that they could see from their location. The stock looked to be in good shape and when he found the pond, it was large enough to provide for the stock and was about three quarter's full after the rain they had received a week before.

July 22nd

We're Going To Walmart!!

Kevin skirted the town until he found the Walmart after leaving the girls and pack horses in a stand of trees about five miles out of town. He watched the area for over two hours looking for any signs of traffic within the town from a stand of trees about two miles from the Walmart store. He moved the girls and the pack horses into this stand of trees just before nightfall and they ate a cold MRE as they watched the town. If anything went wrong Amanda was to take the pack horses and head directly south and they would do everything to evade and catch up to her. She fought the idea, but Kevin put his foot down and she finally agreed once she said she would also take their horses, since they would need them once they caught up to her.

The horses were tied together by their leads and just after full darkness, Kevin and Lavon left by foot for the store. Darkness played in their favor as there was no moon tonight and their goggles gave them plenty of sight as they slowly moved on the store.

At the store, they leap frogged around the store finding the glass front completely destroyed and several of the exterior doors either fully opened or slightly ajar. Since it had rained in this area a week before they found no indication that the store had been recently entered. Lavon waited outside as Kevin entered the store and moved from aisle to aisle then into the back of the store stepping over debris from the store being ransacked. He took note that the food stores were completely emptied as was a major portion of the household and camping areas. The drug store inside had been broken into and it looked cleaned out as was most of the first aid.

Once he was certain it was safe for Lavon, he exited and sent her in. She was working on a short list she had in her head as she went first for feminine products then first aid. She was also collecting things like razors and shaving cream for Kevin and their personal usage. When she had her pack full, she returned to Kevin, exchanged packs and went back in. This trip took a bit longer as she went through the debris that was once female clothing to find underwear and socks. She found six bras she felt Amanda could wear and a couple for herself along with panties regardless of style. She did chuckle to herself when she picked up three thongs in her size and found another three in Amanda's size.

She communicated with Kevin every few minutes to let him know she was alright and that he was also alright. Amanda came up a couple times to let them know she could hear them and she was also in good shape. Kevin had given Amanda his father's night vision scope to observe things in the dark and she was constantly scanning between the town and the store for any movement from her position. Lavon picked up a small school back pack and filled it with things Kevin would consider girly items. She also selected several sets of scissors, sewing needles and thread for repairs to their clothing and found a bolt of camouflage material in the mess. Safety pins and other items for constructing bags were gathered before she had both packs full and told Kevin she was heading out of the store.

Kevin reentered the store and picked up a small duffle as he scoured camping for what was left of the useable items. Once he was satisfied he had all they needed from the mess in camping, he moved into hardware and collected a few things there such as wire clothesline cable and fasteners for it, so he could make a corral for the horses if needed.

When they informed Amanda they were returning, she told them she had them in sight then went back to watching behind them to see if anyone might appear. Kevin tied the bags to the horses and they left as soon as they could because Kevin did not want to linger any longer than they just had to near the town. The rode until mid-morning putting as many miles between them and the town before camping next to a creek. When Lavon went to pee, she took a home pregnancy test kit she had obtained and checked her condition. Her period was a week away and she sighed a bit of relief that she wasn't pregnant. But Lavon knew that it was only a matter of time before she was, and she was not about to refuse Kevin if he wanted her. She was allergic to latex but if he knew she had expended her birth control pills she was certain he would either use a condom or not take her at all. Sex for the two of them was a major stress relief and Kevin did not need the additional stress of having her pregnant. But there was a piece of her that was disappointed that she was not pregnant.

They kept a three on watch cycle and during Lavon's turn, she hid the other test devices in her personal bag. She made bags for her and Amanda's feminine pads and tampons from the material she had picked up then made one for Kevin's shaving gear. Another bag was made for sewing items as she just sat and listened for anything that might be a danger to them. Amanda giggled when Lavon showed her the thongs and later when the girls bathed in the creek, Lavon showed Amanda how to shave so the thong would cover her pubic hair. Lavon reminded Amanda that she was not to wear the thongs where Kevin could see her because she would show much more than she should be showing him at her age.

Kevin got up and bathed as Lavon watched with Amanda in the tent asleep. They enjoyed each other on a saddle blanket before he dressed, and they woke Amanda up for evening chow. After they ate, Amanda studied her first aid manual while Kevin and Lavon tended the horses bringing them down to water. Amanda got Lavon to be a practice subject on a couple of wrapping techniques she learned from the book to insure she had the idea better than the photos showed.

Amanda kept first watch using Lavon's helmet and night vision goggles. She felt safe being able to see in the darkness but remembered Kevin's warning about wearing them too long. She woke Lavon up to take her shift and laid down next to Kevin and quickly went to sleep. When Lavon woke Kevin, Amanda had rolled over away from him, rolled up in a poncho loner. During the last hour Kevin had watch, he brought the horses down one at a time and readied them for movement. He let the girls sleep an extra hour then got them up. Once breakfast was finished and the camp cleaned, they departed on their next leg of their journey.

* * * * * * * * * *

Journal Entry, June 24.

We raided a Walmart in Colorado for items the girls were needing. Lavon has been aggressive when alone and Amanda has been asleep. She has taken more than the load of caring for Amanda during this trip. I don't know what kind of experiences she has had with men, but she certainly knows how to get a man excited and ready. I don't know how long this will last between us but I'm just going to take it one day at a time.

* * * * * * * * * *

They had traveled off the maps that Kevin had and he was having to use a Rand-McNally Road Atlas he had picked up during his first trip into the Wal-Mart to get a sense of location as they traveled. Twice they had to detour to avoid what appeared to be smoke from camp fires in the distance. Kevin maintained his position ahead of Lavon and Amanda in order not to present a large target if someone saw them in a rifle scope or binoculars.

Kevin knew they had entered the Oklahoma Panhandle when they had to cross the Cimarron River utilizing the Highway 385 Bridge and seeing a road marker telling them Boise City was approximately seventeen miles away. He turned due west to avoid Boise City and headed for the New Mexico State line. They spent two days in the Black Mesa State Park using the facilities there for cover as the horses rested. Two days later they were in New Mexico.

August 8th

MEDIC!

Kevin estimated they were three days ride from Santa Fe when he crested a rise, looking down at the wooded area telling there was a creek at the bottom of the valley about eight hundred yards ahead of him. He radioed back to the girls what he was seeing as he slowly moved forward. They had been moving for two days without much water and the horses needed to rest and refresh themselves. He had disturbed a group of antelope as he moved over the crest and wondered what some fresh meat would be like if they stayed an extra day.

He was about halfway down the slope when he first felt the impact of the bullet on his breast plate knocking him backwards in the saddle. He heard the shot from the tree line as his body recoiled back towards the front of the horse and he rolled out of the saddle into the knee-high grass in this area. Immediately his earbud came up with Lavon's voice in his ear.

"Kevin!"

"Lavon, I'm hit in the armor and off my horse. Stay behind the ridge. Unknowns in the tree line about four hundred meters away. Hold and let's see what we have here."

Lavon waved Amanda up and handed her the reins to her horse then dismounted. On the horse directly behind her was the M110 sniper rifle in a soft case where all she had to do was open the case and pull the rifle from it. The magazine was loaded and locked into the rifle. Lavon told Amanda to stay out of sight then she trotted the three hundred yards to the crest of the ridge. She had chambered a round as she trotted up and dropped onto her hands and knees as she reached the crest then crawled over the crest until she had a good view of the small valley in front of her.

She could see Kevin lying on the ground and Tony, his horse had wandered a bit to her right out of the direct line of fire over Kevin. Lavon had to force her breathing to slow as she watched the tree line through the scope after she had adjusted the scopes focus to the range.

"Kevin, I have the SASS and have crawled over the ridge. Amanda is behind the ridge waiting. I see nothing from here right now."

"Hold what you have, but I cannot see the tree line because of the grass."

"Are you hurt?"

"Chest hurts from the impact, but the armor stopped the bullet. I'm alright."

They waited for several minutes then Lavon spotted movement from the tree line. Two men wearing a mixture of clothing walked out from the tree line towards Kevin. She reported this to Kevin and he told her to wait and he would deal with them, but they needed to be within about thirty yards. She only replied understood and thought to herself he had a hand grenade ready for them.

Lavon called out distances as she adjusted the scope for range as they closed on Kevin. The man on her right was casual in carrying his rifle but the man on the left looked nervous and had his rifle in a port carry position as if ready to use it. She was trying to give Kevin good distance reads when the man on the left raised the rifle to his shoulder. Lavon shifted her sights, took what she thought was the proper mil-dot adjustment and squeezed the trigger. She misjudged the range and instead of hitting the man in the chest, she hit him in the bowels. He dropped his rifle and went to his knees and even from that distance she could hear him scream.

Kevin first heard the bullet crack the sound barrier as it went over him and heard the shot almost the same time he heard the man scream from being hit. Kevin came up on his elbow looking towards his intended target and saw one man on his knees and the other standing looking down at him. He threw the grenade as hard as he could then flatten waiting for it to detonate. The grenade flew true, but it only bounced once when it hit the ground, due to the high grass restricting its flight. But it was close enough. When Kevin rose back up he heard Lavon tell him two men down. He pulled his pistol from his vest and walked forward holding his rifle against his body with his left hand.

Both men were dead. Kevin looked up towards the ridge to see Lavon standing with the rifle in her arms looking down at him. He keyed the radio and told them to come on down as he looked around for his horse. Tony had moved off away after the blast of the grenade and Kevin was worried that he might have been hit by some of the shrapnel which has been known to travel as far as seven hundred meters in open terrain. His left arm was hurting from landing on it as he tried not to let the rifle get damaged in the fall and his chest hurt from the bullet impact against the armor plate protecting his chest.

Amanda had only stopped long enough to hand Lavon the reins to her horse before moving down the ridge. When she reached Kevin, she was off her horse with the medic's bag in hand and went to Kevin.

"Kevin, sit down and let me take a look at you."

"Baby, I'm alright, the bullet never touched me."

"Really? Then why is their blood on your left sleeve? Now sit down!"

Kevin sit down, and Amanda went to work removing his vest and armor then his shirt. It appeared that the bullet had fragmented and some of it hit his left arm. Kevin thought the pain in his arm was from landing on it as he hit the ground.

Lavon rode up as Amanda was getting Kevin's shirt opened up and took time to put the M110 back in its case before moving to see if she could help. Kevin winched as Amanda removed his shirt from his left arm then she dropped to one knee looking at his bicep where the blood was coming from. She opened the medics bag and dug into one compartment for the fold out surgical kit, removed the large tweezers from it the very carefully extracted a small piece of the copper jacket from his bicep. She showed it to Kevin before tossing it aside then went back to her bag and withdrew a bandage to wrap the wound.

They helped Kevin to his feet, redressed him then helped him on his horse. Kevin looked down at the creek and decided that they needed to move away from this area because those men appeared to be two hunters which meant others were near and the shots would have alerted any others by this time. He took them back over the ridge and detoured the area, camping out in the open that night near a small pool of water. That night Amanda removed the dressing and cleaned the wound the best she could with the extra items from the medical pack then redressed the wound. Kevin complimented her on how well she had done treating his wound.

That night Kevin had a dream which woke him up. Amanda had come to bed with him and as he slept she enticed him and mounted him as he slept thinking it was Lavon. This scared him, and he moved out of the tent to sleep out in the open as Lavon watched and wondered what had happened in the tent. When she woke him to stand his watch an hour later he told her about his dream and said he would not share the tent with her again unless it was storming. Amanda had not touched him as he slept but this dream concerned him. Lavon told him it was only because for a short time Amanda acted as if she was much older than her years as she was treating his wound.

* * * * * * * * *

Journal Entry, August 9th.

It finally happened. I was wounded yesterday when I was shot by what can only be hunters looking for food but decided that I was a better target with a horse. Lavon took out one with a long shot and I finished the two men off with a grenade. Amanda treated the injury to my left arm that I did not know I had. A piece of the bullets copper jacket tore into my bicep.

But this also created another problem. Last night I dreamed that Amanda and I made love. It's not as simple as I make it sound but it scares me to think about her in such a way. She's only 13 but in my dream, she seemed older and experienced. Hopefully we'll be in Santa Fe in a few days and I can find a safe place for Amanda and Lavon before this gets out of hand and I do something that is just so wrong.

* * * * * * * * *

It would take longer than Kevin estimated as they had to skirt areas with smoke rising from probable campfires. He kept his distance from Amanda when he could, but she insisted on checking his wound each morning and evening. Lavon just stayed back and observed what was happening and did everything she could to relieve the stress she knew Kevin was feeling.

August 23rd

Santa Fe

Lavon guided them to a small farm outside Santa Fe which if the people who owned it would be favorable to them if they were still alive and there. They found a grave in the front yard with a crude marker on it with the name of Cassidy painted on it. Lavon told them that Cassidy was an artist who lived there with her husband who was named Harold. Later after they had moved into the house, Kevin found Lavon out at the grave clearing the weeds from it. He just watched until she had finished and stood looking down at the grave. When she turned to look at Kevin he saw a tear in her eye. She walked to him and kissed him hard then laid her head on his shoulder.

"Kevin, there is something you need to know about me and I want you to be quiet until I am finished. I was studying art with Cassidy when she seduced me into her bed. I was thirteen at the time, the same age as Amanda. Cassidy was thirty-one if I remember right. We were lovers all through school until I joined the Marines. Harold took the rest of my virginity when I was almost fifteen and I enjoyed him often during those years. Many times, it was the three of us in bed playing and getting sweaty. So, I know how easy it is for someone like Amanda to give themselves to someone they admire and love. I have made no attempt to enjoy Amanda as tempting and as easy as it would be. And I'm glad you have not succumbed to her desires."

"Lavon, there was no need to tell me these things. I don't care how or why you lost your virginity or who you have slept with over the years."

"No Kevin, it is important that you know because I was really hoping they were still here, so I could live with them as you moved on."

"Why would you want that? I mean me moving on?"

"Kevin, it is because I'm pregnant and did not want to be a burden on you."

"Pregnant? And you wanted me to move on without you and my child?"

"Kevin, I don't want you to stay just because I am pregnant with your child. My father did that with my mother and it was not a good environment which led me to Cassidy."

Kevin moved her back from him and took her face in both hands.

"Lavon, I have strong feelings for you. Strong enough that I think staying with you and helping raise a child sounds like a great thing to do. But how do you feel about me? Were you just fucking me for fun or were we making love most nights?"

"Kevin, I knew I was at the point of becoming pregnant if we continued having sex without protection, so you think on that a minute. If I was fucking you for fun, a condom works just fine even if I am sensitive to the latex."

"Alright then, all we need now is a preacher unless you just wish to say we are married and go from there?"

"I accept your name and you as my husband if you will accept me as your wife and mother of your child."

"I so swear Lavon I accept you as my wife and mother of my child."

"Well, I guess we are married then which means I can finally say something I have neglected to say for the past month. I love you Kevin Barnes."

"Then I shall say I love you Lavon Barnes because that is all these feelings can be towards you."

"Now Kevin, what do we tell Amanda?"

"Shit, I don't know how to tell her. I think it would be best for you to tell her girl to girl like."

"Okay but you are sitting with me when she finds out."

They went back into the house to find Amanda sorting through the first aid items she had found in the house to add to her stash. Lavon sat her down and told her what had happened between her and Kevin and that they decided to consider themselves married since she was pregnant. Amanda looked at them both for a moment then smiled, before moving to give first Lavon a hug and kiss then Kevin before telling them she was happy for them.

* * * * * * * * *

Journal Entry, August 23rd.

We got to the farm outside of Santa Fe that Lavon guided us too today and Lavon told me she is expecting my child. We decided that we were now married, and Amanda is excited about Lavon being pregnant. Tonight, Lavon and I are going into Santa Fe to see if the people there might be friendly, and we can safely stay in the area. Still not sure what to do with Amanda, but I will not abandon her just to take the pressure off me.

* * * * * * * * *

After they ate dinner, Lavon and Kevin suited up for a night mission into Santa Fe. She knew the town and the people in it and hoped there was still a friendly amount of people to make contact with. They moved Amanda to a place she could hide and not worry about everything around her only what was in front of her. She had the night vision scope plus would have radio contact with them as they walked into town three miles away.

They walked on either side of the road leading into town so as not to give anyone a single target in case there was an itchy trigger finger in town. As they entered the outskirts of the city they came across several burned-out homes. Lavon gave directions as they moved to where her mother had lived only to find the house abandoned. As they moved further into the city they saw flickering of lights from some houses telling them there were people there living by candle light or oil lamps.

Lavon took him further into town and they climbed the fire escape of a building and made it to the roof to look around the city as best they could. There was life in this town but was it a peaceful life or one of outlaws who will kill any new comers to the city? They made a slow circle in this part of town and had to hide in the shadows for a time as two armed men walked the streets talking. They followed the men for a time then broke off to head back to Amanda. On the face of it, those men appeared to be patrolling the streets at night like night watchmen. They collected Amanda then went back to the house to rest until morning.

They knew they could not hide out in this house very long since the only water the horses had to drink was from the Koi' ponds in the back yard. They were using rain water captured in barrels outside the house for their own use and even though they ate MRE's they still had over a month's supply of food that required heating to make it edible. There was an open fire pit which Lavon said had a grate to cook on which Harold often cooked hamburgers on during the summer.

At daylight, Kevin and Lavon was sitting on a park bench in front of the bank in complete uniform of service waiting to be noticed. Both of them had a grenade in hand in case the people that found them were not friendly. It wasn't long before they were spotted, and that person moved away from them. Twenty minutes later four men came up the street walking separated and armed to see who these people were sitting in their town. Lavon commented to Kevin that it looked like they were all wearing badges as if they were police officers even though they wore a mixture of clothing.

The men stopped across the street from them looking at them. One of the men raised his rifle up as if to shoot them and they raised their hands showing the grenades in one hand and the safety pin in the other. Lavon laughed as she spoke.

"Simon Parks, lower the rifle or I'll give you something else to remember me by other than that scar on your left leg when I pushed up off the swings in the fifth grade."

The man lowered the rifle and looked at her with a puzzled look on his face.

"Lavon Kincaid?"

"Yes Simon, Corporal Lavon Kincaid, United States Marine Corps. And this is my husband, Sergeant Kevin Barnes, United States Army. Now we can talk and be friends or we can leave and never bother you folks again, but either way we do this, let's keep it friendly."

"Not very friendly when you have grenades in your hands." The older man commented.

"Sir, we had no idea who would come to meet us or how we'd be met. We've had to kill too many men getting here that wanted what we had and the women with me." Kevin replied to his comment.

"Yeah, there is still an element out in the country that will take what they want by force if they can get away with it."

"I am aware of that Sir. I was shot about three weeks ago, but they did not survive the meeting."

"You were shot?"

"Yes Sir, now may I ask who you are because my hand is getting tired holding this grenade and either I put the pin back in or do I roll it out into the street with you?"

"I'm Clarence Hathcock, and I am the Sheriff here. I guess if you meant harm you'd have already done it. You can replace the pin and my men will lower their weapons, so we can have a friendly talk."

As they were replacing the pins in the hand grenades, the Sheriff told his men to go back to the office and wait there for him unless someone came for one of them about a problem. The Sheriff walked over to them as they stood and offered his hand to both.

"How did a Marine and a Soldier end up married and together to come here?"

"I'm from here Sheriff if you caught that discussion between myself and Simon. Kevin rescued me a couple months back and well, we decided that being man and wife was a good idea considering all we had been through to get here."

"Well the key question is what your intentions are now that you are here?"

"Sheriff, I just want to find a place that is peaceful and start a family. I was heading to my Uncle's place in Colorado, but that area was a battlefield, so we came south to Lavon's home."

"Sergeant, you said women earlier. How many?"

"Just one and she is actually just a kid I found wandering in the woods after her mother and sister had been raped and kidnapped. I was not present to save them, but I did what I could for her."

The Sheriff gave Kevin a strange look which caused Lavon to speak up.

"Sheriff the girl is thirteen and still a virgin. Kevin is a good man and did not take advantage of her situation. So, put any thoughts like that out of your head."

"Yes, sorry, there has been an epidemic of that sort of thing around these parts since those bombs killed the electronics. We hung two men last week that raped a woman south of town. So, where did you two meet, and how did you get here?"

"West Kansas and by horseback."

"You have horses?"

"Yes Sir, we do."

"Can the city make a deal for one or two horses if you have them to spare. In the first month of this disaster, even the horses were being killed for food until the town got their act together and started planning for the future. My Deputies could use a horse or two to get around."

Kevin looked at Lavon who had a smile on her face.

"Yes Sheriff, we have a couple we can part with complete with saddles if we are welcome to stay in the area."

"Sergeant Barnes, be advised I am a retired Navy Chief and only came here a month before the bombs. I could use some more help of the professional type. Those men you saw with me work hard but they are not military or law enforcement types. Would you consider taking the job as a Deputy?"

"I'll consider it next week. My left arm is healed but still a bit stiff and I am just plain tired."

"I can understand the situation. Where are you staying?"

"We are staying at the McCormick place northwest of town. Which reminds me, do you know what happened to Harold McCormick?" Lavon inquired.

"No, I don't, sorry. I've been told his wife's grave is in the front yard, but I haven't been out there. If you want to move into town I'm sure we can find a place. Those that were not killed in the street fighting in those first weeks either stayed or left.

Population is down to around four thousand now. There is still a bit of trouble from time to time but with a meager food supply available now, our trouble comes from out of town."

"Yes, we noticed the patrol last night." Kevin commented.

"You were in town last night?"

"Yes, and not to cause trouble, your patrol was easy to avoid."

The Sheriff laughed.

"From the Combat Infantry Badge sewed on your uniform, I imagine you had very little trouble dodging my patrol. Let's face it, the patrol only keeps the honest folks honest. Maybe you can train my Deputies to do better if you take the job."

"I'll train them whether I take the job or not Sheriff. This is Lavon's home and we intend to make it our home."

"Sheriff, is there any way to find out what happened to my mother?" Lavon asked.

"Once you get settled, I'll have one of my Deputies go with you to ask around about her. Now if you need food, the market will be open in the park in about an hour. If you don't have any money, you can barter for the food. The city council has placed a limit on the amount of food any family can purchase until the crops improve. Meat is in short supply so if you manage to take a mule deer or antelope, you will have plenty of customers to purchase the meat. Now I need to get back to my office and get ready to report your presence to the council. My Deputies will pass the word about you two and that you are not a problem. Have a good day."

"You too Sheriff, we shall talk again." Kevin replied.

As they walked back to the farm they walked side by side talking about their possible future.

"Kevin, you think you'll take the deputies job?"

108

"Honey, it is a consideration. I know how to do three things. Farming, soldiering and carpentry. I'm a fair mechanic with farm equipment but I need to do something to be useful to the community. Anyway, I was thinking that tomorrow, we head up into the hills and see about taking a deer or two for sale. I've butchered cattle and a few deer before. This will also give us an introduction to community."

"I understand Dear, but please do not take any unnecessary chances. We've just found each other, and your child needs a good father like you to teach him how to be a man."

"Him?"

"I can hope, can't I?"

Kevin laughed.

"I always thought women wanted daughters."

"Some do, some don't. Girls can be a hand full especially when they hit puberty as you may have noticed with Amanda."

"I guess in a way we already do have a daughter then. Amanda is going to be a lovely girl and I guess I'm going to have to be the father to her until she finds a man who will take her off our hands."

"Well, we will just have to wait and see."

Just before noon, the three of them rode into town on their horses, leading two of their pack horses saddled up and found the Sheriff's office. Kevin explained they were the horses from the outlaws they had killed at the farm and the town could have them at no cost. Simon Parker had come out of the office with the rest and Lavon asked him if he knew about her mother. Simon said he thought she might have headed south to Albuquerque just after the attack along with a couple other families. That was all he knew because he could not remember seeing her around town after that.

Simon rode one of the horses and took Lavon and Amanda to the open market to introduce them around to the people who were usually there with vegetables and other items for sale. The females received some strange looks considering they were both dressed for combat with their rifles slung in front of them and their heavy vests providing them with protection.

Kevin stayed and talked to the Sheriff about where it might be safe to hunt without running into the groups he had mentioned this morning. The Sheriff suggest the area Kevin had already passed through getting to Santa Fe since he had not seen any smoke from fires the last two days of travel. Kevin had seen deer and a couple of elk as they traveled through the area but left them alone since he was not going to kill something that large for only the three of them to eat for only one or two days.

The girls returned to the Sheriff's office and collected Kevin up before going back to the farm. Kevin spent the rest of the day cleaning out small barn for the horses and looking for whatever he might need to start a new life. He pulled the battery from the old Farmall tractor and put it on the solar charger. There was another shed in the back that had nothing but junk in it which he cleaned out with Amanda's help. Once cleaned out he dug a pit in the middle of it for a fire and figured he would try to use it as a smoker for the meat.

By late afternoon he was tired from the work and the fact none of them had much sleep the night before. Lavon had cleaned the house and they washed themselves in heated water, then washed clothes before bed. As in other farm houses, they rigged trips at the doors to alert them if anyone attempted to break in. They slept till past daylight the next day and Kevin decided to wait another day as they cleaned the place up and took care of the horses. Late in the afternoon, Kevin was able to get the tractor started, but the gas was sour, and it ran rough, but it did run. He drained the gas from several nearby cars and filled the tractors tank, then hooked it to a brush hog and cleared around the house.

Lavon told Kevin that Harold had always kept a sizeable garden and showed him where it was always at. They walked the ground and found several plants that grew naturally and harvested what they could of the vegetables. Onions were growing wild and had seed pods which they harvested the seed pods for the next spring. Everything they picked was overripe, but the seeds might produce something next year if they were lucky. Kevin had over thirty pounds of seed packets he had gathered from various places during their trip which they stashed away for the next spring planting.

The next morning, he left by himself to hunt for deer for meat. He had considered at first taking Lavon, but that would leave Amanda alone. If he took both of them, then everything they had brought with them would be accessible to anyone thinking they could steal it. He was worried about leaving them alone and they were worried about him going off by himself. He told them he would be gone at most three days and kissed them both goodbye as he left before daylight.

* * * * * * * * * *

Journal Entry, August 28th.

Hunting has been good for meat and I have not crossed paths with anyone since I left Santa Fe. It's actually been almost relaxing not having to worry about the girls, even if Lavon is a Marine.

I'm not sure of what is going to happen between Lavon and myself, but I can honestly say I love her. Maybe it's because of what we have gone through which has given me these feelings, and even she has claimed she has the same feelings for me. The only thing we have or had in common was the desire to stay alive and the sex. Now we have a child to bring us together and I think we can make this work. I know I'm going to try and pretty sure she is also.

* * * * * * * * * *

111

Kevin returned as scheduled if a few hours later than he had planned with two mule deer gutted and strapped to the pack horse he had taken with him. He finished skinning them then butchered one in time to take to the market. When the word got out that fresh meat was available in the market they sold out within the hour. Most of their dealings was in barter with one of the other people in the market helping to make sure prices were fair based upon what the council had determined. But as one individual commented, who would think of cheating two females carrying firearms as if they were ready to go into combat.

At home Kevin had butchered the other deer and had it hanging in the smoker. He had sorted through the wood finding the types that would give a decent flavor to the meat and started the smoking process. While that was happening, he cleaned out the fire pit and had pieces of meat on the grate when the girls arrived home loaded down with items they had bartered for to include some fresh vegetables to go with the meat. Everything was cooked outside as Kevin had not given much thought to fixing the fireplace into a cooking place.

Even though there had been fires in Santa Fe during the unrest, it was not burnt as so many other cities had been. Oliver checked with the Sheriff and determined if an item had not been claimed and or the property it was sitting on not claimed, then it was open property for whomever wanted it. Kevin went into the salvage business that very day. He searched all over the city for fuel supplements at any auto parts store that had not been either burnt or completely cleaned out. Tools were important also as he needed them to work on the things he had in mind to rebuild and get running.

Using the tractor, he pulled vehicles into large parking lots and one by one he emptied the fuel tanks into every container he could find and removed the batteries which he recharged using his solar panels. The Sheriff had made him a Deputy which also gave him the authority to do a lot of what he had in mind. He gave the

FRC Radio's he had to the Sheriff along with others he had found for the Deputies to use as they toured the city. They had their limits but at least it was better than nothing.

* * * * * * * * *

Journal Entry, September 5th.

I think I have found my goal in this new life. I'm going into the salvage business. I've also taken a position as Deputy Sheriff which allows me to move around without restrictions. There is so much abandoned property in Santa Fe and if no one is going to recover it, I will and hopefully make good use of it in the future.

* * * * * * * * *

September 8th

The Scrounging begins

Santa Fe was a large city but mostly abandoned during the fighting with the population staying in the northern portion leaving the rest of the city to decay. Kevin moved through the city and suburbs marking locations for future scrounging and was pleasantly surprised when he found the National Guard Armories mostly intact. The weapons vaults had been broken open, but the things not taken were worth more than most folks imagined. It took Kevin a week to figure out how to bypass the electronics on one of the M1249 MRAP Recovery vehicles. It ran rough until he figured out how to adjust the fuel mixture without the aid of the sensors which the EMP had killed.

Kevin remembered something Lavon had said about using the Marine MATV's that had been sheltered inside under a metal roof. He went back into the large indoor motor pool and discovered that the reason the vehicles would not start was because the batteries had been disconnected. Every vehicle in the motor pool started and Kevin had an idea about using them.

He found the radios for the vehicles and outfitted five armored up HUMVEE's with radios and found an RC-292 antenna set along with a power supply which could be rigged up in the Sheriff's office for their use. He took a vehicle to the Sheriff's office and gathered up the Sheriff and Deputies and returned to the Armory to pick up the vehicles.

Kevin remembered working at an ammunition point during one Summer Camp, and thought about how some supply sergeants would substitute once fired brass picked up at gun shows for unfired ammunition not used on a range. He found the office of the units Ammunition Sergeant and after some searching noticed the screws on the return air-conditioning vent had been scratched from being removed.

When Kevin opened the vent, he found ammo cans full of loose ammunition for both the pistols and rifles belonging to the unit. He also found a can of once fired brass for future exchange. Kevin reopened the weapons vault and took out enough pistols and rifles for all the Deputies plus magazines and holsters for the pistols.

He also found hand-held radios which would work after charging their batteries. Soon the Sheriff's office could communicate with all the Deputies. Water was a big concern especially since the nuclear weapons having blown up in such a high attitude had caused the Gulf Stream to push further North and it looked like it was going to be a warm winter with little if any snow. The City Council gave their permission for Kevin to recruit anyone who had skills to assist in the work he was doing. Soon he had a dozen men working with him as he jury-rigged pumps which were then tied to the city's water system. It took three days using the city's maintenance maps to shut off water valves to all but the area needing the water and another two days to fill the water tanks supplying those areas. The residents were told to boil the water to insure it was safe before drinking.

Kevin had rigged a medium size generator to the house and it provided lights and hot water for bathing after he had changed out the hot water tank to an electric one. It ran on diesel and consumed a lot of fuel, but they only ran it four hours a day, in the evening to wash the day's dishes and take showers before bed. The men who assisted him were rewarded with generators and a daily ration of fuel for their labors. Diesel was not as big a problem as gasoline due to its additive mixture and after getting a couple of older model semi-tractors running, they went from truck stops and gas stations pumping them dry until they filled every tanker they could find.

Soon Kevin had thirty men working for him and he found there was more talent in the community than considered. Part of the problem before Kevin arrived was the men were more concerned with finding food then anything which didn't leave much time for exploring or searching for resources. Many also confined themselves to the northern part of Santa Fe after remembering the fighting that had raged in the south.

Lavon and Amanda kept themselves busy as Lavon taught Amanda how to sew and Kevin had provided a small generator to light a single room and two sewing machines along with a fan to move the air around in the house. They would spend hours making clothes using whatever material they could find, and spools of thread then take them every Saturday to the market and sell them. They also made clothes on request since Kevin had taken them to raid every store that might have fabric and thread. Lavon's belly was beginning to grow but she never missed a chance to put a smile on Kevin's face.

Kevin got a shock one day when he came home early and walked into the sewing room to find Amanda standing in the middle of the room only wearing a bra and a thong. He had completely missed her growth spurt and for a second he did not recognize her until she turned and smiled at him. He bolted from the room with the sound of Lavon laughing from what had happened. Lavon came out to find him in the kitchen a moment later.

"What's wrong stud, did Amanda give you a shock?"

"Baby, I was not expecting that. I know I've been gone a lot these past couple months but damn, when did she turned into a young woman? For a second there I thought you were fitting some older girl from town. And where did she get a thong?"

"Kevin, she finally hit her growth spurt thanks to your efforts to keep us properly fed and taken care of. Yes, she is still young, but her body is about par for someone her age. She told me her father was over six feet tall which means she could possibly grow to your height. Honey, the thong is nothing more than a piece of cloth through the ass to protect the vagina. She has been

116

wearing one since Oklahoma and she made that one herself. But do you want to hear something funny?"

"Oh sure, let me have it."

"Your reaction is just like a father towards his daughter upon finding out that she is becoming a woman. So, brace yourself for this. Amanda has two suitors already. Young men that has seen her at the market and now tend to spend as much time around her as they can get away with. One even brought her a flower last Saturday. And she is certainly enjoying the attention."

"Do they know how old she is?"

"Honey, neither of those boys are old enough to vote which means all they see is a pretty young girl. You know damn well what that also means."

"It means they'd love to see her as I just did or with even less clothes on. Christ Lavon, what are we going to do?"

"First of all, we are going to do nothing. I've talked to her about the birds and the bees but considering the relationship the two of you had before I entered the picture she is already well versed in that subject. I just gave her the information that she needs to keep her from making a mistake and finding herself pregnant. If you get too heavy on the subject, she just might go off and do something stupid then be in trouble. We girls are like that when our hormones get in the way of our thinking. Sort of like when a boy gets an erection, the brain stops functioning properly."

Kevin laughed, then pulled Lavon close and kissed her.

"Were your hormones raging when you got like this?" He rubbed her swollen belly.

"No Kevin. I've never told you this but let me try to explain. I was like Amanda when we found each other in that all I had left was hope and it was running in short supply. If you had told me I had to blow you or fuck you to eat, I most likely would

117

have without even thinking about who you were or what you were doing in that creek bed. When I took you the first time it was because you were stressing out and needed to relax. Amanda also noticed that and had even asked me to let you take me the first time she and I were alone."

"She wanted you to fuck me?"

"Yes, she loved you then as she loves you now and felt if you would not take her then maybe by taking me you could relax some. Sweetheart, you are not the best I have enjoyed in bed, but you are the best when it comes to caring. Even when I knew I was out of pills and could get pregnant, I continued to let you have me because it was what we both wanted and for the same reason. Sex allows a person to know they are still alive and have value to another. Its why this child is growing inside of me, because I was more to you than a simple fuck. You cared for me as a person and worried about me as a person. I think you often forget I am a Marine which means I can take care of myself but even Marines need help from time to time and you gave that with no restrictions. Then when I learned I was pregnant I also learned that I had fallen in love with you even if you did not love me."

"Lavon, I never gave it any thought about getting you pregnant. All I knew was that you were giving yourself to me and I was accepting the gift. I should have been more considerate of the possibility. Now can I tell you a secret?"

"Certainly, my husband."

"I never thought I'd survive to see any manner of civilization. From the moment I left my family farm I felt as if I was living on borrowed time. Amanda added to my fears but when you came along, and Amanda refused to go with you, I nearly gave up as I was just worn out inside. Thank you for helping me get here and getting Amanda here."

"Kevin my love, it has been fun for the most part. Those other parts we shall not discuss. Now I have to get back and get Amanda fitted for a wedding dress."

"A wedding dress? But you never said she was getting married to one of those boys!"

Lavon laughed.

"No silly, she is almost the same size as one of the girls in town that is getting married next week. It's a simple dress but will be Karen's wedding dress. By the way, Karen is only sixteen. Kevin times have changed for better or worse and you had best get use to the idea. I know of two girls in town that have children who are barely older than Amanda. They gave themselves, they were not raped. Times have changed whether you like it or not. But I doubt Amanda will give herself to either of those boys no matter how smooth they are. You look at her as if she was a little sister, but she looks at you differently. Her love for you is not brotherly in nature and until she is old enough to realize the difference, she will not spread her legs for some boy no matter how good a kisser they might be. Trust me on this."

"God Lavon, how did life become so convoluted?"

"It became that way when we were looking in a different direction."

Lavon gave him a wet kiss then went back to the sewing room to fit Amanda, so they could finish the dress. As Lavon was pinning the dress to make the finishing touches on it Amanda broke the silence in the room.

"You are right Lavon, I'm not spreading my legs for any boy regardless how good they might kiss."

"Amanda were you listening to our conversation?"

"Yes, because I knew it was about me."

"Amanda that is not a good thing to be doing. What I tell Kevin is for his ears only, not yours."

"Lavon, don't you think I know that? I know you are working for both of us, for our own good and now for the good of the baby, but why can't a man have two wives?"

Lavon stepped back and looked at her amazed at what she had just said.

"Amanda, for one I agree with Kevin. You are still too young even if you are beginning to look like you are much older in form. Get out of that dress and put some clothes on then we'll go someplace where Kevin might not hear us talking even by accident."

Amanda was careful in taking the dress off and dressed before they went outside and walked to a bench under what would be a shade tree in the summer and sat down.

"Amanda, Kevin does love you but something you should know if he has not already told you. His first love was younger than you are now, and they were together until he joined the Army. She took his virginity the same moment he took hers and from the few times he has spoken about her he was truly in love with her. In less than a year after she broke up with him for joining the Army she was not only married but pregnant. I think in many ways you remind him of her and he does not want to revisit that pain again. If it is meant to be then it shall be between the three of us. I lost my virginity in this house when I was your age and I know how dramatic that can be. I also was in love and I still have feelings for that person, but it could never be more than it was. As with you, you may have to move on from what you desire to what is real in life. Only time will tell but I promise you this, I will not stand in the way of either of you if your wishes come true."

"Thank you, Lavon, that means a lot to me."

"But Amanda, I want you to think hard on this. If I understand correctly, Kevin is the only man to treat you with not only kindness but as a person. A person he also loves and respects. A lot of what you feel for him can be nothing more than the mirror image of the reality of both of you caring for each other so many days when nothing was certain. Given time I think you will realize that. When you do I believe your love for him will be even stronger than it is now, but it will be the love of two people who survived the world coming apart and will always be friends but never lovers."

Amanda sat for a minute thinking about what Lavon had said.

"I caught my sister having sex with one of the boys in our apartment complex. I watched as he was on top of her and she was moaning about how good it felt. I remember her face when he finished, and she seemed so happy to have had him in her. She knew I saw her and later I asked her why she was doing that, and she told me that nothing felt as good as when it all comes together with the boy and her reaching their climax at the same time. She said nothing compared to the feelings. I've listened to you and him having sex and can hear the joy in your voice when finished. I hear his also and after all he has done for me, I want to give him those feelings even if they only last for a minute or two. I may have helped him get across Kansas, but he kept me from starving or worse and what I did was little in payment. Am I so wrong in how I feel?"

"Yes and no. You have given him everything he has asked of you. You have even saved his life so that debt is paid in full. You treated his wound as he had treated your insect bites at first. You have cooked and cleaned for him, helped with the horses and took as much load off him as possible. And remember you gave him to me to take care of that which he would not take from you."

"When you gave yourself to him, did you love him?"

"No Amanda, it was just sex. He needed it more than I did but I really wanted a man, any man as long as he wanted me for me, not just a piece of meat. Even from the beginning he never treated me as a piece of meat but as an equal. Part of that was because I am a Marine, but the other parts is because he was raised to respect a woman, even when she was throwing herself at him to get him into bed. Amanda, he took me the first time, so he could kill any secret desires to take you as he took his first love when they were only sixteen. His love and desire for you transferred to me and in a short time I found it easy to be in love with him. Kevin is a good man in a world of evil. Give him plenty of space and in time, we'll see what happens."

"Alright Lavon, I will think on this and I can see the logic in what you have said. Maybe it is because of how he has treated me that makes me love him, but isn't that how love is supposed to work?"

"That's exactly how it is supposed to work. It doesn't always work that way, but this time you pretty well hit the nail on the head. Now let's get back to that dress before we run out of gas for the generator and have to wait until tomorrow to refuel."

* * * * * * * * * *

Journal Entry, October 12th.

I walked in on Lavon and Amanda working on a dress, a wedding dress in Lavon's sewing room today and received a shock. Amanda was only wearing a bra and thong and for a moment, for a long second, I thought she was someone else since she had really filled out since we first met.

My insuring she was eating good and her own genes made her look better at 13 than Gwen did when we first made love when Gwen was 16. I've been gone so much lately that I have missed her filling out and seeing her like that was a big shock. I need to watch myself as I still have feelings for her that I cannot explain.

122

I'm taking a detail back into Colorado to that farm where we buried the weapons and food stuffs to recover them and gather all the livestock we can for the community. I have not talked to Lavon about this but with her being pregnant, I'm sure she will understand about me leaving her and Amanda behind.

* * * * * * * * * *

Lavon and Amanda went back and finished the dress before dinner. Lavon walked into the kitchen to find Kevin looking at the maps he had used to get to Santa Fe. She looked over his shoulder a moment before commenting.

"Kevin, what's on your mind?"

"I talked to the Sheriff and Mayor today. I'm taking a crew back up our route and collect all the cattle and horses we can find. While we are at it, we are going after the weapons and ammunition we buried at that one farm. Plus, there were over forty head of cattle there plus six horses I know of. We need both here if the community is to survive the winter."

"Winter? By now we should have a foot of snow on the ground and it is at least seventy-five outside. When are you planning on doing this?"

"Day after tomorrow if things work out with the trucks we have been working on."

"Then I'd better get packed. How long do you think this will take?"

"Packed? Baby, you're pregnant for Christ's sake."

"Gee, you noticed that, did you? Kevin you're taking trucks which means I don't have to ride a horse plus I can handle the cooking for the group and keep the rations straight for the complete trip. I'm going, and I'd like to see you try and stop me."

"Damn Baby. This could be dangerous. It's not like we were sneaking across fields, we'll be on open roads all the way."

"Dangerous? Then you'll need a medic so I'm going too." Amanda spoke from the kitchen doorway.

"Oh, sweet Jesus. Not you too? Honey I know you have been studying that manual but there is more to it than that. No, you're not going."

"Kevin while you have been working on those truck this past month I have been studying with Patsy Connors. She is an emergency room registered nurse and she has been teaching me three or four hours a day how to treat wounds and injuries. I've also been helping her at the aid station when needed between her teaching me. I may not be up to standards as far as being a combat medic, but I can do the job better than you can right now."

The discussion went on as the girls prepared dinner, through dinner and as the dishes were cleaned. It finally ended when Kevin could no longer defend his position as with every challenge he made they countered to including who would watch the house and care for the horses while they were gone. Under normal circumstances the trip up to the last farm they stayed at should only take a day, but he had allowed for three days and the return home five days. Add another five to eight days gathering up cattle to fill the truck and then home.

Lavon had a four-wheeled drive, diesel powered Suburban to get around in and she would take Amanda with her in it and they would be in the middle of the column during the trip up and back. Everything she would need to prepare meals would be in the Suburban as would the rations. They were also taking an empty fuel truck, so they could pump any fuel they found during the trip and bring it home with them.

The night before they left, they sat at the kitchen table as they cleaned and oiled their weapons and checked to make sure each magazine was full and ready to go if needed. Amanda was up first and had breakfast ready by the time Kevin and Lavon got up to start the day.

October 13th

Back to the Farm

The trip only took a single day with the convoy arriving just before dark at the farm. Kevin left the big trucks out on the road as Lavon took the Suburban to the house. She was also pulling a diesel generator in case the one they had left at the farm would not work but Kevin had it running again within thirty minutes after dumping the fuel from it then replacing it with fuel they had brought. He lite the house up and Lavon fixed hot chow for everyone before they shut down for the night. His drivers kept watch in rotating shifts during the night with Kevin sleeping in the MRAP he had driven up and the girls sleeping in the house.

The next morning, Kevin drove the MRAP to the barn and began to uncover the stash they had left behind as two of the men saddled up the two horses they had brought with them and went to gather up the cattle and horses on the farm. The weapons went into the MRAP while the rations went into the house for the girls to sort through and keep the men fed with. Saddles and other tack was taken from the barn as was grain and hay for the horses and cattle. The big MRAP Wrecker was pulling a water tank, so they could water the stock if need be in the trailers since it was too much trouble to off load them then reload them without proper loading chutes and stock pens.

Kevin had brought Simon Parker with him and he stood in the empty turret of the MRAP with binoculars looking for trouble ahead plus any cattle off in a pasture. They were near the town of Gladstone New Mexico when Simon told Kevin they had people in the road up ahead. As they closed on the group Kevin radioed to the convoy to be careful of an ambush. Before they had left Santa Fe, Simon had attached an American Flag to the MRAP so anyone seeing it would think military and not civilians. Kevin slowed as they closed on the group seeing men, women and children in the group. One man raised his rifle high into the air then laid it down on the road as the other men in the group copied his action.

The convoy came to a stop and Kevin just looked at the people as Simon scanned the area for unwanted guests. Just as Kevin was stepping out of the MRAP, Lavon's Suburban came up and stopped beside him. Both doors opened, and the girls came out with rifles through the open windows aimed at the group. Hands went into the air as the group of people suddenly became scared of what might happen to them. Kevin never said a word to the girls as he walked forward to the group with his silenced SBR hanging in front of him. He stopped ten feet from the group and just looked at them.

"Are you the Army?" He was asked from the group.

"No, but I am a Deputy Sheriff out of Santa Fe to where we are returning if you will let us by."

One man stepped out of the group. He had been the one who had raised his rifle up into the air.

"Is there any way possible that we can go with you? We have maybe three days of food left and to be honest this area is nearly hunted out."

Kevin thought for a minute how he could take roughly twenty people back in the trucks.

"We have a cattle truck about half full. If you can handle the stench, you can ride in that but leave your firearms and knives on the road. You can have them back in Santa Fe. You have my word on that."

Thanks, we can deal with the smell. Do you have a doctor in Santa Fe? We have a little girl who cut her leg a couple days ago and we are afraid it is infected."

Kevin keyed his radio. "Medic Up!"

In just a few seconds he could hear the sound of someone running up behind him, then Amanda stopped next to him.

"What have we got Kevin?"

Kevin pointed to the man who told her about the girl. The girl was brought out and Amanda went to her knees and cut the pants leg off the girl to get a good look at the injury. Amanda stood, pointed to the man and told him to pick the girl up and follow her. The man laid a pistol down he had behind his back and took the knife from the scabbard on his hip and laid it down with the pistol then picked the girl up and followed Amanda. The rest of the people removed all weapons then Kevin pointed towards the rear of the column radioing instructions on where to put them. He had two drivers come forward to collect the weapons and told them not to lose anything, he expected each person to get their weapons back when they get to Santa Fe later that evening.

Amanda had the little girl up in the back seat of the Suburban working on her leg when Kevin walked up to see how things were going. He noticed that the girl had a bottle of water and a sucker in her hands as Amanda carefully cleaned around the cut in her leg. She examined the wound then carefully dabbed the same ointment Kevin had used on her bites on the wound before carefully wrapping it with sterile gauze. Amanda carefully situated the girl in the seat and fastened the seatbelt around her before picking up her things and closing the door. She turned and spoke to Kevin.

"We're going to take her directly to the clinic when we get home. There is something in that wound and we're going to have to open it up some more to get it out before it will start healing."

"Alright. I'll call ahead when we get within radio range and have Patsy meet you there." He looked over at Lavon who was standing in her door watching. "Lavon, get back in line and wait until we are back at the farm before breaking column." He turned away without any further comment.

Kevin was pissed that the girls had broken out of the column and had come forward to protect him but as he thought about it, he had walked out to meet those people with only Simon to cover him. Simon was a good man but untested in his eyes where Lavon and Amanda were tested and dependable. Yeah, he thought, he could get pissed but they had his ass covered if things went sour.

Picking up the group of people cost them over thirty minutes travel time, but he picked up the speed once they were on Interstate 25. Someone took a shot at them as they passed through Las Vegas, but no one reported injuries except for a shattered passenger side windshield on the third truck back from Kevin. The drivers already had their instructions as they drove through Santa Fe to Kevin's farm with Lavon dropping off to head to the clinic. It took till nearly midnight to get all the stock out of the trailers and into the pasture next to Kevin's house with the Sheriff and two Deputies taking the new folks in tow and taking them into town to get cleaned up and housed until the next morning.

The fuel tanker was three quarters full and was taken to a safe location in case something happened, and it caught fire. The drivers ate as they worked with wives arriving and setting up a buffet type dinner. Lavon and Amanda returned to the farm house and just stayed out of the way as they transferred what needed to go into the house that night, leaving the rest until morning. When the last truck was unloaded, Kevin just locked up the MRAP and went in to take a shower and get some sleep. He had told the drivers to take the morning off and he'd meet them at the vehicle staging area when they brought the trucks back in then.

The girls were still up and had showered when Kevin walked into the house. He knew that no matter what he had said about them breaking column and coming to cover him would be a waste of time, so he just kept his peace and cleaned up. As he snuggled up to Lavon in bed, she told him that a doctor had wandered into town while they were gone and had treated the little girl under the watchful eyes of Patsy and Amanda. Tomorrow he was going to check Lavon to see how the baby was doing. Neither of them made sexual overtones to the other as they just snuggled as they fell asleep.

November 20th

A Difference of Opinion

The city council called a meeting and asked Kevin to attend. The meeting had barely started when Kevin was asked to answer concerns about his salvage business. One of the councilmembers thought Kevin's actions concerning the salvaging was not fair to the citizens.

Kevin could barely contain his laughter as he smiled then explained his purpose.

"Council, the city is full of useable items rotting away due to neglect. Now before anyone gets too wrapped up about my side job, the Sheriff can confirm I do not take away from my Deputy duties and immediately respond to any call I am given."

"Now I'm employing forty-two men and women which means they are not sitting around wondering where their next meal is coming from and they are providing a service to the community. I could spend several hours describing what my employees are doing to help the community, but I think you already know that."

"But I want the council to consider this. If you decide that my requiring payment for the goods we salvage is unfair to the community at large then I suggest you take over the business and see how long, it lasts when you cannot pay your employees. Now even though no one is getting rich and we are not gouging the people who need what we salvage, this is something that needs to be done. I'm actually surprised no one considered this before I came here."

Another Council member brought up the fact that Kevin controlled the livestock situation meaning he was profiting from the sale of meats and such from it.

"Council, I employ ten men to take care of that livestock which provides milk, eggs, and often meat that did not exist when I

130

arrived here. It was through my efforts that we had the vehicles, the weapons to protect ourselves while recovering the livestock and the knowledge of where most of it was located that had not already been killed off by hunters searching for food. Has anyone been cheated in the exchange between the consumer and my agents at the market? No, they have not. I wish we could provide more meat to the community, but it takes time for the herd to grow along with the flock of chickens, etcetera. Now from what I understand nearly all of you have a college education yet how is it I had to come to Santa Fe and start what you should have already accomplished?"

No one spoke until Kevin decided he had enough.

"Council, I'm going to let you folks decide what you want and continue with my business. I need to get back out on patrol."

The Council never again brought up Kevin's salvage business after that meeting.

* * * * * * * * *

Journal Entry, November 20th.

I had to lecture the city council today about my salvage business and the fact they all had college degrees, yet it took a simple farm boy to get things started for recovery. Before the bombs, Santa Fe was noted as being a hot bed of liberalism, well maybe that is not fair of me saying that, but it seems they cannot think for themselves at times. To be honest it almost seems like everyone here was waiting for the government to come and rescue them when they had the power to rescue themselves.

I wonder how much of this country is starving as they are waiting for the government to rescue them?

December 25th

Merry Christmas

As usual Kevin was up before the ladies and had placed a couple small boxes under the meager Christmas tree the girls had set up the night before. As he sat at the kitchen table drinking a cup of coffee by the light of an oil lamp he fingered a shoe box that contained what he hoped would be the real present for Lavon this chilly morning.

Through Kevin's efforts the Sheriff's Department now had eight armored Humvee's with radios to use for patrol and response vehicles. The City Council approved the Sheriff's request that Kevin have exclusive rights to one of his own. The reality was that he had three of them complete with radios and was teaching Amanda to drive one of them. Except for a few weapons and all the nine-millimeter ammunition, he kept everything they had stashed at the Colorado farm and paid off the drivers in rations, a few weapons and some ammunition.

The week before Christmas, Kevin had searched the city for jewelry stores that might have something left after all the fighting and scrounging. He found a half-burnt store that had a vault in the back that showed an attempt to break into it but the scaring on the vault door was old, with rust in the marred metal. Kevin spent two days cutting in this vault in the hopes the store owner had moved everything from the store into the vault before leaving the store. He hit pay dirt when he was able to get a hole large enough to look through with a flashlight. He slept in his Humvee that night and the next day emptied out the vault of everything regardless of use or need.

Lavon walked into the kitchen wearing a flannel nightgown with her belly pushing out from it as she was five months pregnant. She kissed Kevin then went about getting things ready for

132

breakfast. Amanda came in a few minutes later wearing pajamas and began to help Lavon. Kevin went out and checked to see that the generator was ready for the day's usage and started it. He had brought a 15KW military generator to the house and had it hooked into the main electrical system. Running it for four hours in the morning kept the freezer and fridge cold as long as the doors were not kept open for very long and gave them cold storage for meats and fresh milk that was coming from a small dairy which Kevin had started using dairy cows he had found on one of his hunting trips.

Kevin sat back down at the kitchen table and made a notation in the notebook he always carried about the fuel he had just put into the generator then looked at the girls.

"Amanda, would you go into the living room and get my journal off the coffee table for me please?"

"Sure Kevin."

Kevin waited for what he was sure to happen since it would be nearly impossible for Amanda not to look at the Christmas tree as she picked up the journal he had left there when he placed the presents under the tree. Seconds later he received the response he was hoping for.

"LAVON! Come here!"

Lavon never looked at Kevin as she quickly walked into the living room. Kevin got up and went to the stove to keep an eye on the thin breakfast steaks Lavon had on the stove and kept an eye on the door for their return. Amanda was the first to come back through the door at nearly a run and jumped on Kevin, hugging him then gave him a very wet kiss which seemed to last longer than it should have. Suddenly Amanda broke the kiss, let go of him and he gently eased her back to the floor. Kevin could see Lavon standing inside the kitchen with a smile on her face as she watched before moving to Kevin.

"Oh, I'm sorry Kevin, I shouldn't have done that." Amanda apologized for her actions.

"Well from your reaction, I take it you like what Santa brought you for Christmas?"

Amanda held up the diamond necklace in the form of an 'A' on a silver chain and grinned.

"Are these real diamonds?"

"Yeah kiddo, they are real and so is the silver chain. It's not much but it is the best I could do."

Lavon held her own necklace up which was shaped in an 'L', and smiled at Kevin. She moved to Kevin and gave him a lover's kiss before putting the necklace on then returning to the stove as Kevin sat back down. Amanda put her necklace on then went back to slicing the bread Lavon had made the day before. Kevin watched her and thought to himself he had to be more careful around her as she felt like a woman as she kissed him even if she was still only a young girl. She was filling out and firming up while the pajamas hid her body as it was developing very well.

Breakfast was placed on the table and they ate and talked about the necklaces and Amanda was telling him how sorry she was that she didn't have anything for him. Lavon just smiled and winked at Kevin which made him slightly blush in that he knew tonight could get interesting even if she was pregnant. Kevin finally moved the shoebox over to Lavon as breakfast was finishing up.

"Lavon, this is in a way part of your Christmas, but I could have given it too you a week ago."

Lavon opened the box and looked at the ring boxes carefully stacked inside of it. She began to lay them out on the table before opening one.

"Honey, I think I got close to your ring size but find the ones you want, and we can use the others for trade and such."

There were tears in Lavon's eyes as she began to open the boxes to view their contents. She never touched a single ring until all the boxes were opened then she carefully selected the ones she liked best and tried them on. Some were single wedding bands while others were matched sets with large diamonds set in them. Lavon put one band on and held her hand out, so she could see how it looked. It was a simple, gold wedding ring that she had selected, and it fit her finger.

"I'll take this one Kevin. It's more than I expected all things considered and it should not be a problem wearing gloves and such. Thank you so very much."

Kevin took a man's gold wedding band from his pocket and put it on. Amanda giggled and clapped as Kevin and Lavon leaned into each other and kissed. She then asked if she could look at the rings which Kevin said she could. Amanda found a white gold ring and tried it on her right ring finger and looked at it for a long time before just closing the box with the ring still on her finger. Kevin and Lavon watched without speaking.

"Kevin, if you will let me, I'm going to keep this one for the day I will need it."

"Yes Amanda, you can keep it."

Amanda stood, leaned over and kissed him on the cheek before she began to clear the table of the dishes. Lavon closed the ring boxes and put them back in the shoe box as Kevin refilled his coffee cup and left the girls to do the chores they had told him were their responsibility. Lavon joined him in the living room later and after a long kiss just held him as tight as she could.

"Honey, you have made this a Christmas to remember. Come with me into the bedroom while I change."

Lavon took her nightgown off, sat on the edge of the bed and crooked her finger at Kevin with a grin on her face. After she had given Kevin his Santa's Helper's Gift, she left him shaking by the bed as she began to get dressed. She was putting on her blouse when she began to chuckle.

"Okay Lavon, what's so funny?"

"I was just thinking about the look on your face when Amanda kissed you this morning. You were most definitely shocked by it."

"Damn it Lavon, why does she do that to me?"

"Because she loves you even if it is still puppy love. Plus, this morning you made her extremely happy. She told me yesterday as she was putting the tree up she was not expecting anything because the way things are right now. Then to give her something as expensive as that necklace, well, even I was floored when I saw mine. I take it you robbed a jewelry store somewhere?"

"Yeah Baby, I did, but it had been abandoned for a long time and half burnt down. The vault was intact, and I broke into that. But your comment about Amanda kissing me brings up something else. For a moment that kiss was not one you would expect from a girl her age. What's been going on while I've been gone during the day and some evenings?"

"Kevin my dear, Amanda is a popular young lady with the boys. Especially when we go to market. The Parker twins follow her around like she was a movie star, and they do take walks together sometimes, one or the other of the twins. I suspect a little making out happens from time to time."

"Is that all? Making out I mean?"

"Honey, yes, that's all I mean. There is only one person that can remove her virginity right now and he won't, so relax.

Besides, she carries a condom everywhere she goes because she has no intention of becoming pregnant even if she decides some boy gets lucky."

"Sweet Jesus, what do I have to do to get her to understand how I feel about her?"

"Nothing Kevin because if you say it wrong or she misunderstands you, one of the Parker boys will get to pop her cherry and I agree she is still too young. Just try to relax and let nature take its course. She is smarter than you think and has goals in mind. Do you know she spends almost two hours a day with Doctor Wilcox studying medicine and she works with him during that time learning all she can to be a better medic if needed?"

"Sorry Baby. I've been so busy answering calls as a deputy and keeping my projects on track I guess I have neglected both of you."

"All three of us understands and we forgive you. Now let's see if we can build a snowman out of that weak layer of snow outside."

The day was spent relaxing and having a bit of fun in the shallow snowfall build a small snowman. At one point, Amanda and Lavon ganged up on Kevin in a snowball fight which he graciously lost when Lavon nailed him with a snowball to the forehead and he just fell over backwards playing dead.

That afternoon Kevin brought in a steer for butchering and spent the afternoon gutting, skinning and halving the carcass for a New Year's Day Barbeque the City Council was putting on. He got the two halves hung up in the smoke house to age and the three of them spent the rest of the day watching movies.

Kevin set quietly as the Parker boys came by bearing small gifts for Amanda. She kept her necklace hidden from them and after she accepted their small gifts, she went to her room and came back with small cloth bags for them. Kevin recognized she was giving them ammunition which in many ways was a very expensive gift these days. She gave both boys a soft kiss at the door as they left and then just came back to the couch and opened her gifts. Both had given her cheap bracelets that she said was on sale in the market. She put a bracelet on each wrist then leaned back to watch the movie.

Between movies when Kevin mentioned how diplomatic the twins were in trying to win her attention her reply was even more diplomatic.

"Kevin, I told them if they wanted my attention then fighting over me was not the way to do it. Until I decide which one will win me over, they must be respectful to each other and share me equally or I will spurn both of them."

"So, do you have a favorite yet?"

"A favorite? Yes. Between them? No."

Lavon put her hand on Kevin's arm knowing he was about to ask a question he really did not want to hear the answer too. Later that night they talked in bed and Lavon just told Kevin once again to let nature take its course. Amanda will make the right decision when the time comes. Kevin stared at the ceiling and worried that if the decision she would make would be the right one for all of them.

* * * * * * * * *

Journal Entry, December 25th.

My gifts to the girls went well. And as simple as their gifts to me was, I really appreciate them. Lavon picked out her wedding ring and I was surprised when Amanda asked for one as she said for a later date. I could not deny Amanda the ring but the kiss she had given me for the necklace then later the comment she made about the 'favorite' man in her life has brought back feelings I wish would go away.

I hope that someday she finds a young man who steals her heart, so I can just concern myself with Lavon and the child she bears.

January 4th

Feelings & An Offer

The barbeque was a success as far as the community was concerned. Kevin had a pit built the week between Christmas and New Years to cook the steer over. It was a pot luck dinner with each family bringing something in order to have enough food for everyone. Lavon had warned Kevin to be quiet where Amanda was concerned, and he really had to take stock of his own feelings when she came from her bedroom dressed for the party.

Amanda was wearing a deep purple dress which fit her form to the point that Kevin swore she was older than her actual age. It hit her just below the knees and she was wearing black nylons and pumps. Lavon had helped her with her hair and makeup which gave her the appearance of a girl much older than thirteen. Everything about her tugged at his feelings which he considered just as strong as he felt about Lavon.

Kevin could not help but watch as Amanda fluttered around the groups of people like a butterfly going from flower to flower. She danced with anyone who asked her, and he saw her give short kisses to several of the boys there. Towards the end of the party she came and asked Kevin to dance with her as a slow dance came up and he held her in a proper manner as they just danced without speaking. Amanda never seemed to make it seem he was any more special than anyone else she danced with and gave him a wet kiss on the cheek afterwards.

When they got home, Kevin's tone was soft as he told her he was concerned about her safety as she seemed so accessible to those boys tonight. Amanda smiled and raised up her skirt to expose her right thigh and removed a switchblade knife stuck in the top of her nylons on the outside of her thigh. She told Kevin no one touches her where she does not want to be touch unless she wants to be touched. Amanda kissed him on the cheek before going to her room and going to bed.

* * * * * * * * * *

Journal Entry, January 4th.

The Bar-B-Que was a success for the community, but I find myself jealous of the boys that gave Amanda so much attention and the attention she gave them. I admit I was also concerned that one of the boys would take advantage of her and take what she is not ready to give. Amanda told me that she was prepared to defend what only one person shall take and showed me the knife she was carrying.

* * * * * * * * * *

Now here it was three days since the party and Kevin was still messed up in his mind why he felt the way he did. He was jealous of all those boys that spent time with Amanda and as he sat in his Humvee, far away from the family, he could only make sense of his feelings in one way. He still had feelings for Gwen and they had transferred over to Amanda. He remembered thinking about Gwen as he first watched Amanda bath herself in front of him.

Kevin had joined the National Guard to serve the state and country while still being able to be with Gwen. Gwen had not only broken it off with him but within months had not only moved in with another man but got pregnant by him. Kevin often wondered if she had not been seeing that man also when they were apart before he joined the Guard. There were a lot of similarities between Gwen and Amanda but as he thought about Gwen he realized she could never have done the things Amanda had done in the months that followed their meeting.

For only the second time in his life, Kevin wanted to run. He was terrified he was going to do something to mess up the lives of Lavon and Amanda. He could not explain why he was in love with Lavon, but he was certain he was. Lavon was pregnant with his child and he was not going to be the kind of father that Lavon had endured but he intended to be one like his own father. As he considered his own father he remembered that Amanda had come from a broken home. Amanda once told him that she never knew why her father had left them, but he had, and she only saw him on rare occasions. Could this be why she was so intent on loving him? Kevin was still confused and scared of hurting either of the females in his life, but he wanted to run. But the first time he was this scared he didn't run. He stood his ground beside the dead body of his teammate and fought against a Taliban attack along with the rest of his squad. No, he wouldn't run but he had to find an answer before he messed everything up between him and the girls.

He was making some notes about one of his projects with the FRC radio in his vehicle broke the silence advising anyone listening there was a convoy of vehicles coming up from the south on Interstate 25. Kevin listened as another Deputy asked what type of convoy was coming and the sender replied it was military vehicles with an American flag flying from the led vehicle. He listened to the conversation and the call up the line to the Sheriff's office alerting them. The Sheriff said he would meet the convoy before it entered the city and would be on location within ten minutes.

Kevin thought about where the best place for him to be based on where the Sheriff said he would meet the convoy. Five minutes later, Kevin was climbing a ladder with the Barret M107A1 and four loaded magazines for it to a high point where he could take the convoy under fire if it was not as advertised.

The Sheriff arrived as planned and Kevin was able to get a range estimate off his vehicle using a laser range finder. After he had the Barret set in place and scope adjusted for range he rolled out from behind it and pulled a brownie from his vest that Amanda had made the night before and took his time eating it as he waited. His personal radio squawked asking him his location and he only responded that he had a visual on the Sheriff with the Sheriff acknowledging affirmative. The Sheriff knew Kevin carried the big Barret and figured he was watching from a location where he had a clear field of fire.

Kevin was still chewing on the brownie when the call came through the convoy was sighted. He rolled back under the big rifle and double checked his range data and waited. Except for his own Humvee, the Sheriff Department's vehicles had been repainted silver with a black star on the sides and hood plus the words Sheriff Department on them to be seen from any direction. Also, the light bars had been removed from standard police cars and installed on the vehicles. The Sheriff had his lights flashing as the lead convoy vehicle approached and finally stopped about fifty yards in front of the Sheriff.

The Sheriff was out of his vehicle, standing beside his door as Kevin watched the turret of the lead vehicle to see if the weapon mounted there depressed to aim at the Sheriff. Kevin had a clear shot at the turret gunner from his vantage point but the gunner never depressed the machine gun mounted as he was observing the situation from that point. The doors on the armored Humvee opened and uniformed men got out and slowly walked towards the Sheriff. All were armed but none of the men made a threatening gesture as the Sheriff moved forward to meet them.

Kevin watched as one man separated himself from the others and offered his hand to the Sheriff. They shook hands then the other man turned and pointed to the people with him as if making introductions. The leader of this group pulled what appeared to be a couple pieces of paper from his vest and handed them to the Sheriff who read them then handed them back. Kevin's radio squawked as he heard the Sheriff issue a stand down order that these were friendlies coming to help. He just watched as the Sheriff turned his vehicle around and led the convoy on into town. Kevin stopped counting at thirty vehicles before he picked his gear up and moved off the roof of the building he was on. The weather might have been warmer than normal for this time of the year, but it was still cold on the building and he was glad to get back into his vehicle. Kevin called in he was available for call and the Sheriff came up and told him to report to the office as soon as possible.

When Kevin rolled into the Sheriff's Department the streets were lined with men and vehicles which watched him roll past. His Humvee was painted flat black with silver markings which made it stand out from the rest. He pulled into his reserved parking space next to the convoy command vehicle and had his silenced SBR in his hands when he exited the vehicle. He was met at the door to the offices by a large Staff Sergeant who looked at him as if trying to decide if he should let him into the offices then stepped out of the way as Kevin just smiled at him. Kevin entered the offices to find a dozen men in uniform standing around and he just moved through them to the Sheriff's office and entered without knocking.

"You wanted to see me Chief?" Kevin always addressed the Sheriff by his former Navy rank.

"I wanted to meet you Sergeant Barnes." The Army Colonel stood and offered his hand which Kevin took.

"Colonel, am I still a Sergeant or a deserter? I never reported to my Guard unit when this shit happened."

"Sergeant Barnes, you and about a half-million other men failed to report for a long list of reasons. All that matters now is that you are serving in the capacity of a Deputy Sheriff. Please relax, any records of your service still existing will be notated in due time concerning your status here."

"Thank you, Colonel. Now as a Deputy I would like for you to clear out some of the people from our lobby and have the streets cleared of troops milling around. If we get a call and I have to hustle out of here, someone is going to get ran over."

The Colonel laughed.

144

"Sergeant Major!" He raised his voice and moments later a burly older soldier entered the room.

"Yes Sir?"

"Clear the lobby of unnecessary personal and have the troops assemble on the sidewalks and out of the street."

"Will do Colonel." The Sergeant Major turned and began barking orders. Kevin never turned to see what was happening because he had experience with Sergeant Majors and once they began to bark, everyone ran.

"Now Colonel, why did you want to meet me?"

"First of all, my name is McAlister, Jacob McAlister and I want to offer you a job."

"Colonel McAlister, I have a job. Several of them in fact. Besides since when do you have to offer me a job when you can order me back to duty?"

"It's because I'm offering Kevin Barnes a job, not Sergeant Barnes. I have been given the authority to appoint U. S Marshall's in areas we survey that need law enforcement. From everything I know about you, you are the man for the job in the Northern half of New Mexico."

Kevin looked at the Sheriff who shrugged his shoulders and shook his head.

"Colonel McAlister, I seriously doubt you have heard all that much about me from the Chief so what gives?"

"Kevin, we have had reconnaissance teams in this area for over two weeks scoping things out while we settled a few problems down in Albuquerque. The reports I received impressed me concerning your intelligence and integrity."

"I wondered who those people were that were moving around the area without just coming in and being friendly. One or

145

two came into the market a few times and others to one of the projects we have going on. One even worked two days at a project before moving on."

The Colonel chuckled.

"They advised my staff that they came and went undetected, but I suspect you were watching them as they were watching you. Interesting. What would have happened if they had done something you considered illegal?"

"Simple Colonel, they would be in our jail right now waiting for you to bail them out."

"And if they had resisted arrest?"

"The ones still alive would have dug the graves of the others not so lucky."

"Kevin, you sound more like an old West Marshall than a modern one. Will you take the job?"

Kevin moved over to the rifle rack and placed his SBR in it then went to the Sheriff's coffee pot for a mixture of coffee and tea since their rations were getting low on both. He sipped the hot mixture wishing it was pure coffee as he thought about the offer. Kevin thought about Lavon and her reaction then about Amanda and his reactions to her and knew he could not run away from the problems he felt inside but this might give him a valid reason for being gone more.

He knew no matter what he did, someone was going to get hurt. Lavon was an adult and had even told him she was going to keep her pregnancy a secret, so he could leave if her friends had still been alive. She loved him but did not wish to be a burden on him. She would understand, but would Amanda? Sooner or later, someone was going to get hurt no matter what he decided.

"I'll take the job Colonel."

146

"Good, let's take care of some paperwork then we can discuss logistics. The Sheriff said your diesel supply was dwindling but I think we can provide for your needs as a Marshall, so you do not have to tap into the Sheriff's resources."

"Yes Sir, I estimate we have about thirty-eight day's supply left and we are mixing diesel with reclaimed cooking oil from restaurants in the area to make that supply go farther. We've pumped out every filling station tanks in a twenty-mile radius and emptied any vehicle we could not get running. Now I have a request for two ambulances which will eat into that even more."

"Amanda?" The Sheriff asked?

"Yeah Chief, Doc Wilcox is going to hold classes for EMT's starting next week. I put my salvage crew on the problem of getting another ambulance up and running as soon as possible. Which reminds me Colonel. We need medical supplies, but I'll let Doc Wilcox handle that request."

"Alright Kevin, have him get with my Medical Officer and we'll do what we can now and transmit a request for additional supplies. By the way, who is Amanda?"

"Colonel, Amanda is a young girl I found half-starved and covered in insect bites on a creek bank in Kansas. I guess you could call her my step-daughter now."

"Yes, I remember an Amanda in the reports. Sort of a fireball about things if I remember correctly. Bright and attractive also"

"Yes Colonel, very bright and at thirteen she looks eighteen. She is untouched, and I intend to keep her that way, so you might want to pass the word for your men to stay at arm's length of her."

"Mister Barnes, that look on your face says a lot such as you'll kill the man who tries to hurt her."

147

"Colonel, she killed a man up in Colorado that was about to kill me. And I would have killed you out on that highway if anything had gone wrong during the meeting with the Sheriff."

The Colonel looked at Kevin for a long time before he just nodded his head in acceptance of the situation. In his mind, the Colonel was remembering the location of the highway meet and realized that the nearest building was over a half mile away if he judged right. Kevin must have been on top of the building with a very high-powered rifle if he could make that statement watching the meeting. Yes, the Colonel thought, he had picked right. Sergeant Kevin Barnes was just the man for the job ahead to help bring peace back to this country.

As things progressed with the paperwork and getting Kevin sworn in as a U.S. Marshall, he was dreading going home and telling the girls what he had done. But that problem took care of itself when Lavon and Amanda showed up at the Sheriff's office as Kevin and the Colonel's Logistics Officer were hammering out a few minor details on getting supplies into the area. Lavon did produce a letter from her last Commander detaching her from duty, so she could return to her family which she had kept in a plastic bag. Once again, the Colonel explained that she had no worries concerning her absence from duty and that in her current condition was exempt from recall.

Lavon's attitude was it was still his life and he had to do what he felt was best for them and the community. Amanda seemed to be excited that he was now a Marshall instead of just a Deputy Sheriff, and that through him the community was going to get some help, especially in the medical side. Kevin had talked to Doc Wilcox about Amanda since she was spending so much time at his elbow learning how to treat injuries and just basic medicine. Wilcox told him that Amanda had a knack for what she was learning, and suggested Kevin support her in this endeavor since so many children just goofed off since they had no goals other than to stay alive till the next meal.

The convoy moved to the old New Mexico Military Department grounds and set up bivouac for their stay in the area. The new state government was being set up in Albuquerque, and no one knew if it would return to Santa Fe. Lavon had told Amanda to avoid the soldiers since they could be crude and not knowing her age might make suggestions that would be inappropriate for a girl her age. Amanda said she had been approached by several of the young men in the area concerning such suggestions and she had no plans to surrender the one thing they all wanted from her. She was reserving that for someone very special someday.

It was when they all were home that things changed for Kevin. Lavon waited until they were in bed before bringing up the subject, so Amanda would not hear the conversation.

"Alright Kevin, what is this all about? I know something has been bothering you since the barbeque and I think it is about time we talked about it."

Kevin lay looking at the ceiling before rolling over to look at her. He unloaded his feelings concerning her and Amanda adding how he had felt about Gwen, so Lavon would hopefully understand. Lavon never commented as he told how he was feeling and his desire to escape a situation where either of the women he loved would be hurt. Except leaving would hurt both of them which he just could not do. Taking the job might help get him away from time to time but it was also a job that needed to be done.

Lavon listened to him with a tear in her eyes knowing he did in fact love her with or without the baby growing inside of her. She still felt her initial judgement of him was correct in that he was a good man, maybe too good for these times, but still a good man. She listened to him describe his feelings for her and Amanda and thought how messed up he really was inside. Gwen had hurt him deeply and now, he was afraid of being hurt again and hurting someone else as he was hurt. Lavon knew he was right when he talked about being killed in the line of duty so the people he loved would understand his leaving. No, he was not going to put himself into that situation on purpose, but the reality of it had to be addressed and accepted.

She finally decided that he had to do what was right for all of them, even if it seemed wrong in so many ways.

"Kevin, maybe this is wrong but get yourself out of our bed and go sleep with Amanda. Tell her how you feel, how you really feel before she thinks her own dreams will never be accomplished. I'm not telling you to go make love to her, but hold her and tell her how you love her. She needs to hear that before she makes a mistake she will regret for the rest of her life. I love you Kevin Barnes and I love Amanda also. Go make her happy because I seriously doubt she is regardless of what it looks like on the outside. Go."

Kevin rolled over and kissed Lavon long and soft before rolling out of bed. Inside he was scared to death to do what she told him to do but he also felt she was right. They had all gone through so much together, more than a lot of people who survived the months following the event. He took two steps towards the door then turned back and put his pajama bottoms on since he slept in the nude then he picked up his pistol to have by the bed if he in fact did stay in her bed.

He crossed the hallway and knocked on Amanda's door and waited. He knocked again a minute later, and she called out it was okay to enter. Kevin entered and closed the door behind him which was something he had never done before and walked to the foot of her bed. The oil lamp beside her bed was burning and the glow make Amanda look years older than her age. He didn't know where to start so he just started with Gwen and told the same tale he had told Lavon minutes before.

Amanda sat up in bed, pulled her comforter covered knees up to her chin and listened to him explain his thoughts and feelings. Kevin even told her about how jealous he had become watching her enjoy the company of the young men at the barbeque. When he finally finished, she just sat and rocked on the bed as she considered his words before speaking.

"Thank you, Kevin, for being so open and honest with me. I've had a lot of time to think about us, you and me. Lavon is most likely right in that the feelings we have are probably because of what we have shared over the past months. When I first offered myself to you it was because I was starving, and my body was the only thing I had to offer to pay for food. I was terrified of being hurt by being used for sex but my desire for something to eat was greater than my fear."

Amanda moved off the bed and stood beside it. Kevin could not help but notice she was only wearing a t-shirt but was unsure what she had on underneath.

"Kevin, I have tried hard not to be a burden on you, but I also put myself in position several times during our travel to allow you to use me because I had nothing but that to repay you with for what you were doing for me. You were hardly sleeping and tense nearly all the time. Looking back, I probably caused some of that tension. Since Lavon joined us, you relaxed more and slept better. I'm too young to comment on whether it was the fact that Lavon is a Marine and capable of helping us stay safe or the sex the two of you started having. Maybe it was a combination of both, but regardless of my feelings towards you I am very happy for the both of you."

Amanda pulled off her t-shirt and Kevin looked away from her.

"No Kevin, look at me. I'm only thirteen and I have a better body then girls much older. My mother barely stood five feet and had large breasts and my father was over six feet tall. I'm

151

almost as tall Lavon and certain to have another growth spurt in a year or two. I've done a bit of reading about the biology of a female and even though my body tells people I am ready to breed, have sex, we both know at my age, the mental side is just not ready."

Kevin looked at her as she turned around twice then put her shirt back on.

"I love you Kevin, and if you want to take me tonight, I won't fight you and will try to please you, but we both know it's still too soon. I know that Lavon will not stand between us if you wish to make love to me, but I think we should hold off, stay as we are until I am older because I understand now that the animal desires of two people are often conflicted by the moral conscious. Go be with Lavon. I'll be here where you are ready, and it is time for us."

Kevin walked around the bed to her, took her face in his hands and softly kissed her lips. Amanda never touched him as he kissed her, she just stood and returned the kiss. Kevin stepped back from her and smiled.

"Amanda, if you find a boy you wish to be with, I'll not stand in the way of it as I want you to be happy. Right now, I'd be lying if I said I would not be jealous, but I really do want you to be happy even if it is with another."

"I know Kevin and believe me that I will follow your wishes if there is a boy out there for me. Now go to Lavon as this is hard enough on both of us as it is."

"Amanda, you are wise beyond your years."

Kevin gave her another soft kiss then left her standing by the bed. As soon as he closed the door she threw herself on her bed and cried. Part of her tears was from knowing that Kevin did love her, but the rest was from knowing she was causing him to doubt himself, to be in a distress because of her.

Lavon looked up at Kevin as he walked back into their bedroom and smiled at him.

"Lavon, what are you not telling me?"

"Darling, I'm not telling you a lot of things because it is for you to learn them as all men do. We females can be illogical with our feelings and it drives men crazy. Relax lover and come back to bed. In time both of you will have what you want even if it not what you think it is now."

* * * * * * * * *

Journal Entry, January 8th.

Yesterday was interesting. I am now a Deputy U.S. Marshall in charge of Northern New Mexico. Lavon is accepting of my new job and Amanda is excited for me. This will give me a reason to be gone more and away from Amanda, but it makes me guilty as hell. Lavon caught onto my feelings and after a long talk she sent me to be with Amanda. She sent me to make love to Amanda if that was what Amanda wanted. I can't fight both of them and I do love both of them. Amanda told me that she was not ready for me and to return to Lavon until she is ready. To be honest, except for my jobs, I think Amanda is more mature than I am. Amanda made some good points about why we feel the way we do about each other. Maybe time will adjust those feelings as we grow older and realize it was just a passing thing because of the horrors we experienced together.

February 19th

Kevin's Birthday

Today was Kevin's birthday and as he looked down at
Lavon still asleep he remembered how lucky he was to have found
her. He went and checked on Amanda who now left her bedroom
door open and found her uncovered laying cross ways on the bed
with her pantied rear exposed in the moonlight coming through her
window. Kevin gently covered her up and went to make coffee.

He sat at the kitchen table by lamp light and remembered
the morning after he had talked to Amanda. Amanda said she
would date when asked, then told Kevin to relax about her dating
since her virginity solely belonged to him and she had no intention
of letting a boy touch her where she had not allowed him to touch
her. She then kissed Kevin as if they were lovers before she went
to fix breakfast. This confused Kevin but also calmed his concerns
for her being out and about in the city, often alone.

During the first week of his new job as the U.S. Marshall
for the region he went out to the outlying settlements and contacted
them letting them know that law and order was returning even
though some folks bucked up against the idea of having law
enforcement stopping them doing what they wanted too.   He
explained they had two choices: deal with him or deal with the
Army since the country was still under martial law.

Colonel McAlister had left a short Infantry Company to
provide assistance if needed in the outlying areas and he had taken
three up armored Humvee's along with him with their turrets
armed and manned. They now had a modified phone system
running from Albuquerque to Santa Fe and in time each settlement
would have a line to the Sheriff's Office in Santa Fe.

Eight days later, Kevin responded to a rustling report from one of the settlement's that had radio contact with Santa Fe. He tracked down the rustlers who were just about to shoot the cow which had been providing milk for the settlement's children and butcher it. He tried to make it simple for them, but they started shooting which ended with two rustlers' dead and one wounded. Kevin had taken a hit in his left shoulder which was mostly soft tissue damage but had earned him a stern lecture from both girls about being careful and having back-up on the scene.

He returned the cow with his shoulder bandaged the best he could by himself along with the wounded rustler and another cuffed in the back of his Humvee. When he called in that he was enroute back to Santa Fe with two wounded and then had to advise he was one of them, he found both girls waiting for him at the clinic. Doc Wilcox stood back as he had Amanda treat his wound until he had to step in and do his own work on Kevin's shoulder. Kevin watched as Amanda worked quickly and without emotion on his shoulder but once the Doctor said he was ready to go home once his IV of whole blood was drained, Amanda unloaded on him with tears in her eyes.

Doc Wilcox gave Kevin a shot for pain and Lavon drove him home while one of the Deputies brought his Humvee home. The girls stripped him down for bed and they both slept with him in the middle. That was the only night he had both girls in bed at once and he was too doped up to appreciate it. Two days later he was back out in the country responding to calls with an Army Corporal driving and another one backing him up while his arm was in a sling.

Kevin was drinking his morning coffee while working a stress ball in his left hand building it back up from his injury. He also had a twenty-pound dumbbell which he would use once he squeezed the ball fifty times.

Amanda came in, kissed him then went to get things ready for breakfast. Part of Kevin's pay now came in the form of rations provided by a weekly supply convoy from Albuquerque. This morning they were having ham steaks and eggs along with orange marmalade. Each week he submitted a request and if the items were available they were shipped up to him. Amanda was sipping on a cup of hot cocoa when Lavon finally made her appearance. She was seven months pregnant and the doctor warned her to be very careful having sex for the next month and no sex after that until after the baby was born.

The Army had installed three phones in Kevin's house which if he picked one up it would automatically connect with the Sheriff's Office dispatcher. One was in his bedroom, one in the living room and the other in the kitchen. He stood and picked up the kitchen phone and when it was answered, he advised he was up and available for call but would be at home until otherwise notified. Kevin intended to take his birthday off if possible.

After breakfast Amanda changed the dressing on his wound and checked to see it was healing properly with the exercise he was doing to keep it from stiffening up. Amanda cleaned around the wound and then kissed his shoulder near it before bandaging it. Lavon sit quietly during this process as she watched Amanda carefully yet quickly worked at a skill she was developing in medicine. When Amanda finished and had her first aid materials put away, she walked back to Kevin, closed his legs and straddled him, wrapped her arms around his neck and kissed him as if she was about to take him right there at the table. Lavon giggled as she watched since they had not exchanged such passion before. When Amanda broke the long kiss, she leaned back and smiled.

"Happy Birthday Kevin. What would you like to do today if they do not call you about a problem?"

"How did you know it was my birthday?"

156

"I looked at your Army ID Card when you were showering back at the Colorado farm." Lavon replied for Amanda.

He laughed.

"I guess that's fair since I have seen yours too. Wouldn't it be interesting if the baby is born on your birthday?" He commented.

"Yes, that could be interesting. Amanda, would you like to get off my husband's lap and go get the box please?"

Amanda laughed, kissed Kevin again then hopped off to run to her bedroom. A minute later she brought back a plain cardboard box and set it on the table in front of him and then sat down on the opposite side of the table from Lavon. Kevin opened the box and smiled.

On top of the items in the box was a new razor and a pack of blades for it. A bottle of Brut After Shave still in the box along with a can of Gillette shaving cream. Next was a pair of new wool socks. The other items were a package of ink pens, a small notebook, and other sundry items. Kevin knew they had to have gathered these things up for weeks if not months to give him for his birthday and he felt as if these simple things were the best birthday present they could have given him. He put the things back in the box, stood and moved over to Lavon and kissed her before going to Amanda and doing the same thing then thanked them both for the gifts.

The day was relaxing for the most part as he only had one call in the late afternoon. One of Kevin's responsibilities was in dealing with the interaction of the civilian population and the Army garrison. Any complaint filed by either party had to be dealt with by him and both sides found he was careful in not taking sides and digging for the truth of the matter. This dispute was nothing more than a Soldier showing maybe too much attention to a girl whose boyfriend took offense and took a swing at the Soldier.

Kevin had to give the Soldier credit for only restraining the young man instead of fighting back. When he finally got down to the root cause, Kevin found out the girl was trying to get her boyfriend jealous, so he might marry her and used the Soldier as her pawn in the game.

The Soldier admitted that he was only interested in sometime between the sheets with the girl and had no interest beyond that. Kevin gave him the name of a young woman who was known to entertain men and sent him back to his unit. He then talked to the young couple for several minutes advising the young lady that she could have gotten her boyfriend seriously injured and that if she cared so much for him, she should have told him so. He then told the boyfriend to get a grip on his temper before he finds himself in the clinic being put back together by the Doc. He notified the Garrison's Commander that he would drop off a copy of the report tomorrow and that the Soldier only acted in self-defense and controlled the situation in proper form until someone in authority could arrive.

The Santa Fe community continued to grow as some people returned or new people arrived to start life all over again. Electricity returned as did natural gas service. Much of the city was in ruins from the fighting that had taken place in the first months of the blackout and many of the projects which Kevin had started expanded in cleaning up as much of the mess as possible. The outlying areas around Santa Fe slowly became calm as the new state government helped arrange for food and supplies enter the region. It was still a rough go, but the survivors had been living on less and Kevin had to deal with less and less complaints as time moved on. He was a stickler for graft within the system and twice jailed support managers who were overseeing the delivery of goods for trying to price gouge to line their own pockets.

One manager even tried to bribe Kevin which failed because unknown even to Lavon and Amanda, he had built a small fortune from raiding the remains of jewelry stores and banks before he became a Marshall. The girls knew of the large amount of money they had found at the Colorado Farm in the weapons vault and had used that money from time to time to buy things at the market they needed being careful in letting anyone know they had more than enough money to survive on. Kevin had taken care of his project supervisors and even was partners in projects suggested by others and was becoming richer with each passing day. He could not be bribed with money or gifts, even a few offers of sexual favors. Kevin was wealthy but insured the funds went back into the projects to insure the men working for him were paid and they had what they needed to handle the projects. His ideas of salvaging every small item possible for future use was paying off for him and the community.

April 22nd

A New Addition

The anniversary of the 'Event' came and went without fanfare as the people of Northern New Mexico went about rebuilding their lives. The Native American tribes living in this region were found to be more self-sustaining and had survived better than the rest and had only taken up violence when it encroached upon them. Kevin visited with the tribal elders as often as he could and had made deals for cattle and sheep to restart ranches outside their tribal lands. The tribes came to respect his authority as he would often turn over one of the tribal members over to the elders to deal with except in the rare case of rape or murder.

Kevin was up at Farmington when the call came over his radio that Lavon was in the clinic due to her water breaking and was in labor. Since this was a social call to see if the small Farmington Police Department needed anything, he broke off his stay and headed back to Santa Fe. Lavon was in labor for twelve hours as he sat by her side holding her hand with Amanda acting as attending nurse, taking her pulse and blood pressure after each contraction. Kevin opted out of going into deliver with her, but Amanda was there and assisted in the delivery.

Carl Wayne Barnes was born at 0347 on April 23rd weighting six pounds, nine ounces. Lavon named the baby after Kevin's father. There were no complications with delivery and Lavon was in good spirits when she ran Kevin and Amanda off to go home and get some sleep since there was nothing more they could do as she also rested.

Kevin was up in Taos investigating a shooting when Lavon was released from the clinic to come home with the baby. Sheriff Hathcock drove them home to be greeted by Amanda who had been working hard getting the nursery set up and ready. When Kevin finally got home at two in the morning, he found Amanda sleeping with Lavon and the baby sleeping in a basinet at the foot of the bed.

He showered in Amanda's room then went to sleep in her bed so as not to disturb them. He had hardly gotten to sleep when he was awakened by the baby crying and when he went in to check on him, he found him in Lavon's arms as she was just getting ready to breast feed him. Amanda smiled at Kevin, kissed him and told him she was going to her room now that he was home.

* * * * * * * * * *

Journey Entry, April 26th.

I have a Son!! Carl Wayne Barnes! He was born on the 23rd but this is the first chance to make a journal entry since then. Lavon and Carl are healthy and at home now. Amanda is being a great help in caring for the baby taking a load off Lavon. Like Lavon he has a dark complexion but has my blue eyes.

June 21st

Birthday's

Lavon's birthday was celebrated on April 29th along with a baby shower given by some of the women in the community. Little Carl seemed to take it all in with the normal attention span of a six-day old baby. His world revolved around sleeping, filling his diapers and drinking from Momma's nipple. Amanda would talk to him about how his diaper stank as she often changed it for Lavon especially during the baby shower.

Kevin surprised both girls when he suggested they have an actual birthday party for Amanda and she could invite whomever she wanted to it. Amanda invited a dozen youth's she often associated with and Lavon commented to Kevin during the party that it was a fifty/fifty mix of male and female.

The patio area of the house had been cleaned and a few extra lights rigged for the party and Amanda had picked out some music for dancing in the open area. Carl was brought out when Amanda blew out her candles, but Kevin and Lavon mostly stayed indoors to give her that time with her friends. Amanda did tell Kevin before the first guests arrived to not concern himself with what she did tonight because she was not sleeping with any of her guests. Kevin had a puzzled look on his face as Amanda bounced off to get ready and Lavon chuckled. She told Kevin that Amanda was known to kiss a girl as quickly as she would a boy and no, neither of them had engaged in any form of contact except for what he had already seen when he was away at night.

The party lasted until after ten in the evening and Amanda insured each guest had a good time. She helped clean up after the party then said she was going to shower before going to bed. Kevin had given her a Breitling wrist watch for her birthday, but she had not worn it during the party. She did receive several hand-made bracelets and two necklaces from her guests.

November 16th

Setting Things Straight

Kevin returned from a month in Wyoming leading a platoon of Infantry chasing a group of outlaws who had been rustling cattle and had killed a couple of ranchers with two bullet holes in him. One wound was to his left leg and the other a flesh wound to his side where there was no armor protection from his vest. The outlaws were better armed than the intelligence on them had reported and Kevin was wounded when he left cover to drag a wounded soldier out of the line of fire.

The girls took turns sitting with him at the new hospital in Santa Fe while a surgeon was brought up from El Paso to work on his leg with a second operation. Lavon told him that when he was able, she intended to get pregnant again. This was too close a call and she wanted another child, someone for Carl to play with and grow up with. Amanda seemed withdrawn, but they did talk about the new school that had opened back in August and her studies both in school and with Doctor Wilcox. Kevin had a lot of influence in setting up the school and the teacher's understood his reasons in that math and science will get a child further in life than liberal arts. Also, he demanded that a true history was taught not some retouched version as had been taught prior to the event.

All the way back into Spring, Kevin had one of his salvage teams collecting books from abandoned houses and businesses for a library to replace the one that had been destroyed and burned during the fighting. He never understood why people would do such a thing because a library only provided knowledge but unless a book fell off a shelf could do no harm. Kevin even taught carpentry once a week in the afternoon when he was available which often meant the class might be held on Tuesday one week and Friday the next week. He arranged other craftsmen to come in and teach in order that skills outside an office would be learned.

It was during his month long stay in the hospital that Kevin also carefully divorced himself of most of his projects, turning them over to the men and a few women who had been managing them for him with him keeping a modest income from the businesses. Carl was a month old when Kevin had taken a large sum of his money and opened a Savings and Loan office giving people a place to put their meager savings and to loan money where needed.

Early after their arrival to Santa Fe, Lavon noticed that even those empty houses that had been raided for food, there was a large amount of flour and other needs for baking left untouched. She had Kevin gathered every pound of flour that could be found and then had a wood fired pizza oven built in which they could bake bread. The bread was sold from the store front and when the Army arrived, arrangements for a supply of flour and baking soda was arranged. Soon there was enough bread baked each day to supply the community and the Army garrison, along with a few cakes and other baked goods. Kevin figured they were making at best a dime a loaf of bread, but it paid for the flour and wages while giving them a modest income to improve the bakery. When power was restored, they moved locations to an actual bakery once the broken windows were repaired and they increased their ability to produce baked goods to include donuts on a limited basis.

The first two nights after Kevin was allowed to go home, Lavon made the most of it while insuring his leg was not harmed. The wound in his side had healed to the point he was stiff but not in any discomfort. Lavon was working hard to become pregnant again.

Kevin had the two Corporals that assisted him appointed as Deputy Marshall's and they dealt with any problems that arose while he was recovering. Lavon had exercise equipment installed in the house just before Carl was born and Kevin was using it daily to rebuild the damaged muscles in his leg since he was somewhat restricted to the house until the Doctor's released him to limited duty. Lavon took advantage of the situation with being home during the day while Amanda was either in school or at the hospital studying with Doctor Wilcox.

Lavon was doing everything she could to become pregnant again to the point that Kevin was beginning to complain about the amount of sex he was having. Unknown to Kevin and Lavon, Amanda had convinced Doctor Wilcox to put her on birth control without notifying them because they were never legally placed as her guardians. Wilcox considered how many girls her age had become pregnant since his arrival and arranged with the Army Garrison to have birth control pills as part of his monthly medical supply shipment.

It was late January when Lavon was confirmed pregnant. Amanda seemed delighted but both Kevin and Lavon had noticed something bothering Amanda for over a month. She had placed a television in her room with a DVD/Blu-ray player and except for checking on Carl from time to time or playing with him in the late afternoon, she kept to her room studying and she always kissed Kevin, Lavon and Carl goodnight. Lavon finally broached the subject she was almost afraid to ask of Amanda while Kevin was down in Albuquerque as the arresting officer in a murder trial.

"Amanda are you pregnant?"

"God no Lavon, what makes you ask such a thing?"

"It's the way you have been acting lately. I know Kevin doesn't care if you are a virgin or not, but if you are pregnant that changes everything."

"No Lavon, I am not pregnant, and I still have my virginity."

"I'm sorry to bother you then but Kevin is worried about you and so am I. We've came to far not to talk to one another if we have problems."

"Lavon, I've been watching my friends party, enjoy each other and at the same time arguing and fighting over each other. I'm the only one not having sex and after seeing some of the problems it has brought my friends I'm not sure what I want anymore. But also, not sleeping with Kevin often hurts deep inside. I'm afraid that he won't like what he gets once he takes me or I will not like what he gives me when it is all finished. I suddenly find the whole mess distracting and I'm afraid if I let him take me then I will not be able to focus on my studies. Lavon, I'm just plain scared of having my fantasy and it not being what I thought it would be."

"Amanda that's the problem with fantasies, they are often more than reality can provide. Honey, Kevin is not the biggest or the best lover I ever had but because I love him he is all I need to make me happy. I can't even imagine making love to another man because of the way I feel about him. Amanda in a normal life this relationship between the three of us could not exist. Not without a price to be paid by one or more of us. I've told you about the people who lived here and my relationship with them but the price that was paid for my love of them was my virginity and if I loved them I feel they didn't love me the same way. I was seduced into a lesbian love affair which ultimately led to Harold taking the rest of my virginity with the three of us often sharing the same bed. I've had both male and female lovers over the years but now I am so happy with Kevin the thought of a female lover has never crossed my mind."

Amanda just looked at Lavon for a long time as tears began to roll down her cheeks. Lavon went to her and sat down beside her and held her as Amanda cried. Neither spoke for a long time until Amanda finally stopped sobbing and once more spoke.

"Lavon, I have never allowed a boy to touch me. My breasts or my vagina. But they have been touched and I enjoyed it."

"Another girl?"

"Yes, another girl. It has only been once and only a couple weeks ago."

Amanda removed herself from Lavon and went to her dresser, opened a drawer and reached in the back of the drawer under her clothes and produced a DVD which she brought to Lavon to look at. It was a hard-core porn movie.

"I found that a couple months ago and have been watching it late at night after everyone has gone to bed. I promised myself that only Kevin would touch me, have me and I've kept that promise but I became intrigued with watching two women make love to each other on that and wondered what that felt like as long as nothing but maybe a finger found its way inside of me."

"So, Amanda, what did you learn?"

"I learned that I enjoyed it more than I thought I would and now I am afraid I'll enjoy Kevin taking me more than I can deal with and maintain my studies with a clear mind and not wishing he would take me again."

"Do you want to have another lesbian experience or was once enough?"

"This is where I am confused. If the situation presents itself again I will have it but no, once was enough in that I am not going out to find another lover in that fashion."

"Amanda the only thing I can tell you is that Kevin will not be upset by you having that experience. I have withheld nothing about my previous sexual life and he has told me that the only thing that matters is the future not the past. Kevin is not going to think any less of you if you tell him about that one sexual

168

experience. But there is no reason to tell him either. Your virginity will be evident by the blood on you, him and the sheets once he takes what only you will allow to be taken. Amanda, you are smarter than your age should be and yet still confused about how to live life even after what you have seen and done. If you want Kevin, take him and get it over with. But remember the first time may not be all your fantasy has made it out to be. You have a part to play in the fantasy and until you learn your part you might find disappointment for a time then it will be all you every wished it to be."

They talked for nearly an hour until Carl woke up from his nap and wanted his mother. Amanda put the video back in the dresser then went back to her studies feeling a bit lighter now that she had some of her guilt off her chest and a better understanding of what she needed to do.

When Kevin got home, Amanda asked if they could talk in private. This bothered Kevin in that she had never asked for a private talk before. They went to Amanda's bedroom and she closed the door behind them.

"Kevin, I have some things to tell you but please wait until I'm done before commenting."

"Alright Amanda. Go ahead."

"Kevin, before you get upset thinking I am having sex with a boy, forget it. But in case you are not aware of it, I spend a lot of time at the Commune doing medical checks on the kids there, especially the babies."

Kevin knew about the Commune. It was an old elementary school building that was being used by orphaned youths as a living space and meeting place. He had never had to respond to a call there as it seemed the kids maintained an open society and never bothered anyone. But he had heard stories about the sex between the kids with some as young as twelve.

169

"Amanda, now I'm worried about your safety."

"Don't Kevin, since I am always armed when there and I have already taught a couple boys what not to touch. Kevin, they have rooms where if a couple wants to have sex, they just go and do it. It didn't take long before the boys understood I might kiss them, but I was not going into one of those rooms. One boy learned the hard way with a knee to his balls after he tried to grope me."

Kevin laughed at how she said that.

"Anyway, I wanted you to know about that and not to worry about me since it can interfere with your job. I'll soon be fifteen and the more time I spend with those kids I realize that becoming sexually active at this age is not only distracting but has the potential of making a great mistake. I delivery condoms to the Commune almost weekly but girls are still getting pregnant even though Doctor Wilcox will provide them with pills."

"Amanda, I only want you to be happy. Listen, I have never said this out loud but if it had not been for you during the first part of our trip here I just might have given up and just stayed where I was at and let nature take its course. I was tired, exhausted but when you joined up with me I had you to consider. Saving you was the biggest success of that time."

Amanda walked over to Kevin, took his hand and sat on the edge of her bed and pulled him down to sit next to her.

"Kevin, people are always talking about Karma, do you think that Karma set this up for us to be together? What are the odds you and I would find each other in that location? Out in the prairie, miles from anywhere. Then for Lavon to find us in much the same way. If there is a guide, someone guiding Karma then I would like to believe he gave us to you because you are such a good man. So please relax your concern about me, I'll let you know if some boy attracts me long before they are allowed in my pants. Right now, I have other things on my mind that I know has you worried because you do not know what they are. In time you will learn, and I hope accept the decisions I am making for myself right now, but I do still love you."

Kevin pulled Amanda's hand up and kissed it.

"Amanda, as I have said many times before, I only wish you happiness."

She leaned over and gave him a short, soft kiss before they separated with Kevin leaving to take care of the things he had to do as she picked up her books and turned to her studies.

May 23rd

Another Addition

Kevin got a shock in late May when an Army transporter arrived with his old work truck on it, with the heavy tool boxes still intact. The new local government in Kansas had made an effort to ensure that the property recovered or salvaged was returned to its rightful owners and when his name came up as a serving U.S. Marshall, they contacted the Army and had it returned to him. The transport driver had no knowledge of what had happened to the people in his apartment complex, only that he was to bring the truck to him. Kevin still had the keys to the truck and tool boxes in his nightstand. He turned the truck over to his vehicle salvage crew who had it back on the road in less than a week.

The Marshall Service kept him on the road a lot that spring and summer, but he managed to get home for Amanda's birthday and brought her a nice evening dress he had found while up in Denver. Lavon adjusted the fit and she wore it for her birthday party they held two days later, on a Friday night.

Lavon gave birth to another boy in late October which she named Walter Conrad Barnes. She also had the Doctor fix her, so this would be the last pregnancy for her. She told Kevin two was enough for her and if he wanted any more than he had best get busy with Amanda. Kevin stayed the course in that Amanda was not only still too young, but a child would hamper her other dreams of becoming a doctor. Amanda was standing back from them as they discussed this and just smiled knowing he did love her to the point her dreams came before their passion.

Down On The Border

Kevin was watching the activity across the border into Mexico through a high-powered night vision scope mounted on a tripod. Mexican bandits had been entering the United States much in the same way Pancho Villa had and he was there to stop it.

The Deputy U.S. Marshall for Southern New Mexico was in the hospital with three bullet holes in him from trying to do what Kevin intended to do this night. The difference was Kevin had brought help in the form of two Army Infantry Rifle Platoons and two Light Mortar Platoons.

He had arranged for a Mexican-American Deputy Sheriff to go south of the border to watch for such activity, so he would know when and where to set this ambush on the bandits. Kevin had to shake his head at the brazenness of the bandits as they gathered on their side of the border as they prepared to cross where the old border wall had been destroyed and removed during the attempt to retake this area back under Mexican control.

Even though the remains of the wall could be clearly seen through the scope, infrared markers had been attached to the remains so there would be no mistake on Kevin's part that the bandits had in fact crossed into the United States. Standing next to Kevin, looking through another night vision scope was the Army Lieutenant in charge of the mortars ranging the group and passing on the information to his Fire Direction Center to insure the mortar rounds would not be wasted tonight.

Behind Kevin stood the Infantry Company Commander waiting for Kevin to order open fire by his Infantry which had moved in just after dark and dug in positions. They were in a large semi-circle configuration which allowed overlapping fields of fire into the fire sack that they bandits would be pushed into by mortar fire if everything went as planned.

The bandits were gathered and preparing to cross the border in cars and trucks along with some horses. It was just after two in the morning when the first vehicles began to move to the border. Their movement was slow considering those on horseback, but they were coming as if they were not afraid of being hindered. Kevin could see men standing in the back of the first vehicles, trucks, as they were ready for a fight not knowing they were ill prepared for the fight they would be soon involved in.

The bandit column was about a quarter of a mile long and soon the last of them had crossed the border. Kevin had eight 81mm mortars available to him and two of those mortars would be used to close the border, firing only at the gap in the border wall to prevent the bandits from just running back to the Mexican side. The others would be controlled by the Mortar Officer as he desired to push the bandits into the Infantry's Fire Sack.

Kevin stepped away from his scope and surrendered it to the Infantry Commander, so he could control his troops fire. He knew that the mortars firing on the border were firing at maximum range, so it would take some time before this dance would begin. Kevin released control to the Army and just stepped back out of the way.

The Mortar Officer was talking to his Fire Direction Center giving adjustments when there was a long pause then Kevin heard him give the command fire. Nearly three hundred meters away the first rounds went out of their tubes to seek out flesh and bone.

It was a full moon and Kevin put his binoculars to his eyes to watch what could be presented through them as he waited for the first rounds to impact. The first rounds impacted just to the left of the column, to the west of them and Kevin heard the Lieutenant give and adjustment. More rounds were fired as Kevin saw the first rounds impact on the border to insure they had the range.

The column first moved away from the impacts as predicted and even with normal binoculars, Kevin could see men

174

being thrown out of the backs of trucks from the impacts of mortar rounds sending shrapnel into the column.

Suddenly the entire area was lite up as one mortar was firing Illumination shells with their flares hanging from parachutes, slowly drifting down on the rear of the bandits, back-lighting them for the Infantry.

The third volley of mortar rounds impacted along the column as they panicked. Men on horseback were being shredded as were their horses from the shrapnel from the mortars along with the vehicles in the column. Kevin heard the Company Commander issue the order to open fire and suddenly tracers could be seen crisscrossing the fire sack and light machineguns opened fire. What could not be seen was the thousands of bullets ripping across the terrain from Infantry rifles.

There were muzzle flashes from the bandits as some tried to return fire but those lasted only seconds as they attracted the attention of riflemen and snipers. Within minutes the vehicles of the column were on fire and Kevin could not detect any movement of the desert floor below them from his vantage point on a ridge.

The ambush lasted at best three minutes before the command to cease fire was heard and the Infantry and Mortars ceased the destruction within the fire sack. The only weapon firing was the mortar firing the Illumination rounds to keep the area lite up.

Kevin just watched as both officer searched with their scopes for movement before the Company Commander ordered elements of his Infantry to enter the Fire Sack to look for survivors. The Infantry carefully left their positions as the machine gunners and snipers watched for movement within the area that might be hazardous to the men moving forward.

As the Infantry moved through the destruction left by the mortars and their own fire a shot could be heard and a radio report telling everyone that a wounded horse had been put out of its misery. Then reports of wounded began coming in. Trucks, hidden from the bandits moved in to pick up the wounded for medical treatment. This was one thing Kevin demanded once the shooting stopped.

Two hours later, Kevin was standing in front of the survivors of the ambush. Some were in serious condition and might not last till daylight but had been given the best care the field medics could provide. There were seven walking wounded amongst the survivors.

Using the Deputy Sheriff to speak for him since Kevin did not speak Spanish, he told the walking wounded that they could return to Mexico but if they ever returned he would insure they were hung from the nearest tree or sign post. The more serious wounded would be taken to a hospital and given care and returned to Mexico once they were well enough to travel.

Kevin stated that if there was ever another attempt by bandits to cross into the United States he would not be as generous and allow the Army to completely destroy any group desiring to raid into the United States and any survivors would be hung without trial.

At daylight, two civilian cattle trucks moved into the Fire Sack and the dead were loaded into them after their bodies and body parts were placed into body bags for transport back to Mexico for the Mexican authorities to deal with.

Kevin had utilized the Army in this because the country was still under martial law, but the Mexicans did not have to know that soon the martial law edict would soon be lifted. Except for some smuggling and rustling of cattle, never again did bandits cross the border.

Another Promotion

Kevin's reputation in dealing with problems caught the eye of the Governor of New Mexico and called him to Albuquerque to talk to him about heading up the State's version of the Marshall Service. Kevin privately admitted to himself that things had quieted down in the north and his two Deputies were handling things in a manner no one could challenge. He asked for the outline of the charter that the State House had to vote on and approve before accepting the job and took it back to Santa Fe to dissect and comment on.

He found one part where the State Marshall Service would be the dominate legal authority over tribal lands within the state which upset him. Kevin had worked hard at getting tribal police forces set up and supplied so they could deal with their problems without interference from outside the tribe. Kevin wrote that a mutual assistance pact must be approved by the tribal councils before the State Marshall Service had any jurisdiction within tribal lands except for the pursuit of a known or suspected felon.

Kevin returned the charter to the Governor and spent a day explaining his changes to him then another day standing before a joint session of the House to get his points across. The charter was voted on a week later and passed both Houses by nearly an eighty percent approval. Kevin was sworn in as the Chief Marshall of the New Mexico Marshall's Service a week later with Lavon and Amanda present.

As before Kevin soon found himself in a situation where people thought they could purchase his favors only to be sadly disappointed. Eight months before he took the job as head of the Marshall's Service, the State had passed a flat tax, so they could pay the bills. Kevin had an auditor come in and audit all his business holdings to insure a proper accounting would be made when he paid his taxes. The auditor went over the books of every company or business Kevin was earning money from and was surprised that if anyone was skimming or hiding funds, they were better at it then he was in finding it. Kevin was not surprised because as one of his managers once told him, they would have starved without the work to pay for food. His managers kept faith with Kevin as he kept faith with them. Kevin wrote a check from the Savings and Loan for two point three million dollars to the State of New Mexico.

Kevin was authorized twenty Marshall's to start with and Kevin spent two months interviewing and hiring his Deputies. He did circumvent his own requirements concerning agreements with some of the tribes by hiring three members of Tribal Police onto the Marshall's Service. After some searching he found five men with Forensics background and went back to the State House for the funds to hire them and purchase the equipment for them to do their job. When each man was hired, Kevin told them if at any time they had the need for extra money to come to him. If someone out in the public discovered one of his men had a special need for additional money it could become a situation where bribery could come into play. His terms were simple, a dollar for a dollar payable when possible with no other strings attached. This put his men above the temptation of accepting bribes or special loans which could hamper their assignments.

Kevin was not at home as much as he would like and even considered moving the family to Albuquerque, but Amanda was moving forward in her education at a rate which amazed even her teachers. She had a real knack for Chemistry and Biology with Mathematics not far behind. She was studying Anatomy with Doctor Wilcox and even assisted in some surgeries if she was present at the time scheduled. Doctor Wilcox figured that by the time she was twenty she could sit for her medical boards.

The relationship between Kevin and Amanda stayed as it had been since the beginning knowing that to do more than just kiss from time to time was even a bit risky. But as Amanda was approaching her eighteenth birthday, he noticed her kisses seem more mature and even sexual at times even if they were short. Kevin finally asked her if she was seeing someone else off to the side and she admitted that she was in a loose lesbian relationship but one that was not important to her except to explore her own sexuality. Amanda told him that she enjoyed the experience, but it only relieved her own desires until it was time for them to take the next step. She swore she was still a carnal virgin and it was still his for the taking when she was ready.

* * * * * * * * *

Journal Entry, April 19th

Amanda and I had a long talk about her sexuality. Damn, even writing this it feels wrong, but it was an interesting conversation. I was afraid she had gotten herself into trouble from the way she had been acting but she told me she was still unknown to the male of the species. She has a girlfriend that she plays with when she felt the need for sexual relief.

This was not something I ever considered but I honestly can accept. If Amanda desires to continue as a lesbian, then all I can do is support her as she moves on through life. She'll soon be eighteen and she has come a long way since she walked into my camp a scrawny, insect eaten creature.

Lavon has told me long ago that they had not had sex since Lavon is bi-sexual, so I hope that whomever Amanda is enjoying is safe, disease free. Why did I just write that? Amanda is studying medicine and working with the youth of the community to help them through the medical problems they have. Certainly, Amanda is sure that she will not contract some disease which could derail her own future.

Damn, I just went from worrying that Amanda might be pregnant to worrying about her getting some social disease. I really need to relax, she knows what she wants and according to her, I'm it. She is a beautiful, young woman and it would be easy to take her. Is it wrong for me to have these thoughts? I have decided that it is no longer a matter of moral conscious but one of desire. Lavon knows how I feel about her and Amanda. Now is it wrong, based upon how civilization is still reeling from the effects of the bombs to consider a man having two wives? I mention that because I cannot just take Amanda to bed, even if she is willing.

179

* * * * * * * * * *

What Amanda did not tell Kevin she was also seeing one of the Corporals from the Military Police unit now stationed in Santa Fe. Kevin went back to his office at the capital and put Amanda's situation out of his mind since there was nothing he could do now and wasn't sure it was his place to do anything about it.

Amanda came home late one evening from a movie date with the Corporal. Lavon had reopened the one theater not destroyed during the uprisings, so people could have something to do in the evenings at a price of ten cents a person. She was up with Walter who had an upset stomach when Amanda walked into the kitchen to get herself a glass of water before going to bed. Lavon noticed there was a stain on Amanda's blue blouse and went to her as Amanda stood by the sink. She rubbed her finger against the damp mark on Amanda's blouse then put the finger into her mouth.

"Amanda, is this wise?"

"Lavon, my hymen is still intact, but I will not lie to you that I'm having a hard time waiting for Kevin to do something about us."

"Honey, Kevin will not get all upset if you give yourself to the young man, but please be careful."

"Lavon, I've watched several porn videos and see things that has me wondering about myself. I've not allowed Tim in my pants, but it seems if we make out for five minutes he has an erection trying to tear through his pants. So, I am giving him some relief while learning how to hopefully make Kevin happy when the time comes. Lavon, I am confused as hell because it really excites me, and I orgasm when he does. Is that normal?"

"No Amanda, but it does happen. As I said, please be careful."

They went to bed not knowing that at that very moment Kevin was in Ruidoso working a hostage situation. Three smugglers had taken refuge in a family home when the local police had interrupted their exchange of the drugs they were carrying for money. Kevin had flown down in the helicopter his department had received via a grant along with two of his Deputies.

Kevin walked out from the protection of the vehicles in the street and moved onto the lawn of the house, so he could speak with the smugglers without yelling. He was slowly learning Spanish and tried to talk the smugglers out as his men had taken positions to kick in the door and enter.

When he announced who he was, one of the smugglers yelled out in Spanish then opened fire on him. Kevin was hit twice in his body armor then once in his right shoulder as he was going down. His men took the door and killed the shooter as the others threw their guns down and raised their arms in surrender.

Kevin was told as he was being treated by a Paramedic that the man who had shot him said that Kevin had killed his father several years ago along the border just before he opened fire. Kevin may not have fired the shot that killed the smuggler's father but had given the order. He just lay on the gurney and thought about how things often come back around on a person.

Lavon had barely gone back to sleep when the phone next to the bed rang. She rolled over and picked it up knowing that the dispatchers would be aware that Kevin was in the Capital and it had to be emergency which scared her.

"Lavon here."

"Lavon, this is Rod Levin in Dispatch. Kevin was wounded about thirty minutes ago trying to talk some smugglers into surrendering after they had taken a family hostage. The wound is non-life threatening and he is on his way to Albuquerque via helicopter now. There will be a car in the morning about nine to take you to him."

"Thank you Rod. Please keep me posted if there is any change."

"No problem Ma'am."

As Lavon was placing the phone back on its receiver, Amanda spoke from the door.

"How bad is it Lavon?"

"Kevin was shot again. Rod says it is not life threatening and he is on his way to the hospital." She spoke as she sat up in bed.

Amanda moved to the bed and crawled onto it and hugged Lavon as they both quietly cried over Kevin being wounded. They held each other for a long time then Amanda moved to give Lavon a kiss as she had done a thousand times before but this time it lingered until it became a kiss of passion shared between them. Lavon had a flannel nightgown on while Amanda was only wearing a pajama top. Amanda finally broke the kiss and looked at Lavon before she opened her top and then leaned back into Lavon who met her with her own desires.

They slept together, wrapped up in each other's arms until the alarm clock woke them. They shared a shower and decided that Kevin did not need to know about what happened between them for the time being. As they were drying each other, Amanda told Lavon she would stay with the boys while Lavon went to the hospital to see Kevin. Lavon could tell that Amanda was conflicted by what had happened between them and her activities with Tim as she still professed her love for Kevin.

"Amanda, you have to make up your mind. You know Kevin loves you as much as he loves me but like you, he is confused about that love. You and I have avoided what happened between us for a long time but we both knew it was bound to happen, and I for one really enjoyed the time together."

"Lavon, I remember a long time ago on a creek bank that you said you would rather make love to me than Kevin. Yes, I've avoid this because I didn't know how you'd react."

"Well, we know now don't we. Honey, we spend a lot of time alone with Kevin gone, so come to my bed anytime you want. But I have to ask you something I maybe should have last night. When you are down on Tim, blowing him, is it Tim you see in your mind, or Kevin?"

Amanda blushed as she dropped her head down looking at the bathroom floor.

"Kevin."

"I thought so. Listen, in my opinion if you continue with Tim and give in to him before Kevin comes to his senses and takes you to bed, I think all the time Tim is making love to you all you will see is Kevin and that would be unfair to Tim and yourself. When that happens, you will feel a guilt that you could avoid. Give me some time to work on Kevin for you, alright."

"Alright Lavon. Now we'd best be getting dressed before your ride gets here. Please tell Kevin I love him."

"I will Amanda."

Both were still nude as they closed to each other and exchanged a long, passionate kiss before Lavon went to get dressed while Amanda returned to her room to get dressed. They exchanged a light kiss before Lavon left for Albuquerque. Amanda sat with the boys and thought about what Lavon had told her and decided that Tim would have to wait for his pleasure since she had long ago promised it to Kevin.

When Kevin awoke he found Lavon sitting next to the bed where she could look at him. His shoulder ached, and he knew he

183

was in trouble from the look on her face. His throat was dry and asked for water which Lavon helped him with. Once his throat felt close to normal he just looked at Lavon.

"Alright my love, speak your mind."

"Kevin Barnes, you are the director of the chief law enforcement agency in the state. It is no longer your job to go into the field to put down trouble. You have a wife and two children to think about plus a wonderful girl who is waiting for you to get your head out of your ass."

"Baby, I'm still a bit groggy, care to explain that last part?"

"Amanda is almost eighteen meaning she is old enough now for you to finish what started on that Kansas creek bank five years ago. If you can find me another eighteen-year old virgin in Santa Fe, I'd be surprised. So, get healed up and finish this before some boy comes along and both of you make a mistake."

"Alright Lavon, tell me how I can do that? And why is it so important now?"

"It's important because she is seeing a young man that is close to getting what he wants. So, either you get well and take her to bed or tell her to take her young man to bed and end this once and for all. I love both of you and I hate to see what is happening between the two of you. Kevin, your morals were fine when you first met Amanda, but they no longer apply."

"Lavon, but wouldn't that be cheating on you?"

"No. Simply because I am telling you to do this."

"Lavon, let me think on this. And going back to the beginning of this conversation, I heard from the Governor before I went into surgery. He pretty much said the same thing about keeping my ass out of the field and if I do go out there, let my men do their job as I sat back and observe and advise. And I'm giving you the polite version."

Lavon stayed until noon then went back to Santa Fe to tell Amanda about Kevin's condition. Amanda was thrilled to know that Kevin would not suffer any loss of movement in his shoulder from the wound and should be home in a week. She told Lavon that she had given Tim a lot of thought during the day and decided that she was going to back away from him to give Kevin a chance to wake up and come to her bed. Lavon told Amanda that she had talked to Kevin, but he was still confused. Just give him time to see the light at the end of the tunnel.

Later that night after the boys had gone to bed, Amanda looked up from her books to see Lavon standing in her doorway nude. Amanda smiled, put her books up, took off her t-shirt and threw the covers back on her bed.

* * * * * * * * * *

Journal Entry, May 1st.

Well I'm home from the hospital after taking a hit from a gunshot. Lavon came to me in the hospital and told me to get my head out of my ass and take Amanda to bed before she makes a mistake with another boy. Dear Lord I have been avoiding this for years and now Lavon has stepped in to shove it in my face. Do I love Amanda? Most certainly. Do I want her happy? Of course. Do I want to see her go off with another boy? I think it would break my heart if she did even if it was best for her. And I think she would not be as happy as I would like her to be if she did.

I'm stuck with a dilemma in that is it proper to have a wife and a lover in the same house? The three of us have come so far together and Lavon is probably right in that I need to finish what was started in Kansas when Amanda offered herself to me for food. But now it would not be for food but for love.

All I have to do now is find a way to make this happen without just dragging Amanda to bed since I think that would be the wrong way to accomplish what needs to be done.

* * * * * * * * * *

Lavon stepped in a week later and made a suggestion to Kevin that at first floored him then accepted it as a great idea. It was accepted that they were man and wife yet at no time had they exchanged vows therefore in a real sense they were only common law partners. Both knew there were rumors about Amanda's status within the family since it was well known she dated, but refused to even enter into light foreplay with the boys she went out with. She had even set the Parker boys up with other girls which one had already married and the other was not far behind him. Lavon suggested he legally marry Amanda once she turned eighteen.

Two weeks before her eighteenth birthday, Amanda stood for a fitting of a wedding dress after Lavon had told her she had a commission for the dress. Lavon would ask Amanda what she thought of the dress at each fitting and if Amanda suggested something, Lavon changed it to meet her suggestions. It was a strapless dress showing plenty of cleavage and Lavon had it fitted one breast size larger knowing she could quickly adjust that before the wedding.

Kevin discussed the situation with the District Judge who agreed that legally he was not married and could marry Amanda if all parties agreed to the marriage. He arranged for him to meet with Lavon who explained it was her idea and she fully supported a marriage between them. The Judge did ask the delicate question of how long they had been having sex and Kevin told the Judge if there is a medical test to prove Amanda's virginity, then she would take it without questioning their reason. The Judge told Kevin that it was not important as it was more a personal thing since he felt Kevin to be above average in his ways of doing things and he would have hated to find he was the same or even weaker than men who professed their high standards. Kevin did tell the Judge they had slept together when she was younger and why, but that Amanda had no carnal knowledge of him and she had sworn she had none of any other male on the planet.

The afternoon of her birthday, a party was held with all her friends gathered around enjoying the weather and snacks. Kevin had told her she would have her present from him after the party and by nine in the evening the only people left was just the family. Kevin's present was a set of diamond wedding rings which caused Amanda to break down in tears but what really shook her up was when Lavon brought out the wedding dress in its box. Kevin told her unless she wished to file a complaint, he wanted to marry her tonight and they had a judge standing by to perform the ceremony. She all but jumped into his arms then hugged Lavon before taking the dress to her room with Lavon following.

When Amanda emerged wearing the wedding dress, the Judge was present, and Kevin had changed into a suit. Kevin had to admit that she was beautiful as she walked to them and he winked at Lavon who was smiling from ear to ear. The ceremony was simple and over before it they knew it. They kissed afterwards, then Lavon took Amanda back to her room to help her out of the dress and prepare herself for her wedding bed. Lavon asked Amanda if she was ready for the final step and Amanda told her she had been ready for months, she was just waiting to see how Kevin could deal with things. Lavon laughed and told her that she was the one who had suggested this marriage and how it would not affect their relationship other than now, Amanda had equal rights to Kevin which they would worry about next week after the honeymoon.

Lavon also told Amanda that this is what she has been waiting for and to not hold anything back tonight. She said to relax, enjoy the moment, and to not rush in losing her virginity.

"Lavon, do you think Kevin will be upset if I go down on him?"

"Honey relax. Just do what feels right and enjoy yourself. But be prepared, Kevin has a great tongue."

187

Amanda giggled then leaned over and kissed Lavon before running her off, so Kevin could take over. Lavon went to Kevin and told him Amanda was ready and reminded him she had been on the pill for several years now waiting for him.

When Kevin entered later, he undressed as he viewed Amanda standing at the foot of the bed in a black, see-through nightie. Once nude he stepped over to Amanda, untied the nightie and pushed it off her shoulders before pulling her close and kissed her. Amanda felt as if she was going to explode as she felt his manhood twitching against her stomach as it was becoming erect. But when he reached around her and grabbed her by her buttocks and pulled her tight to him, her moan of pleasure was loud.

Kevin moved her to the bed and sat her down on it then kneeled in front of her. As they kissed he pushed her onto her back then worked his way down her body as he also spread her legs and moved in between them. When Kevin finally reached the one place she wanted him, Amanda seemed to explode as her body reacted violently to the effect of him down on her. Lavon smiled as she lay on her bed listening to the sounds coming from Amanda's room through two closed doors.

He tormented her as long as he felt was necessary as she was tearing at the sheets from his treatment of her. Deep in her mind she knew that of all the experiences receiving sex in this manner, she was feeling greater orgasms than ever before. Kevin stopped and rose up looking over her and rubbed himself against her. Amanda shook from knowing that he might take her virginity in that position and was barely able to get out a no, not yet from her strained throat.

Kevin moved onto the bed with Amanda and turned her on the bed as they kissed and touched each other. He started to move between her legs and she stopped him, pushing him over on his back. Slowly she worked her ways down his body until she was where she could take him with her mouth. Kevin was shocked at first at her proficiency in performing oral on him, then remembered some of the rumors he had heard concerning her. Her hymen may be intact, but her mouth was far from being a virgin. He just laid back and enjoyed her performance on him until he had to tell her to stop before she triggered his climax.

Once again, they moved about the bed kissing and touching each other until Kevin found himself in the one position they both wanted him in. She pulled her legs up and waited for Kevin to take what was left of her virginity. His push into her was slow as he tore her hymen apart with her crying out with pleasure and digging her nails into his back.

Kevin wanted this to last as long as possible, but the passion between them was such that soon he was driving himself into her as she was crying out with each jarring stop at the bottom of the thrust. When he felt himself releasing into her he cried out which triggered Amanda's climax. Lavon listened to the cries of pleasure hoping that they would not wake the boys as she knew what had started in Kansas was finally consummated.

He took her twice before exhaustion finally forced sleep upon them. In the morning he was awakened by Amanda taking him with her mouth. He just laid back and enjoyed the feelings as she took him all the way to his climax. He told himself that the blood on the sheets and what they washed off each other as they showered before the second go before sleeping confirmed her vaginal virginity which meant she had never given herself to another even if her mouth was well skilled and experienced. Kevin decided to never bring up her ability to perform, to just enjoy it and move on with life.

The first week was a honeymoon set up by Lavon in that Kevin was to sleep with Amanda nightly and even take her anytime during the day he wanted her. He even took her to the Capital when he had some paperwork that could not be put off and they stayed in his small apartment that night. Kevin made no demands on her but tried to supply her with everything she asked for.

When they returned home near the end of the honeymoon week Kevin put his foot down concerning how he would try to take care of his wives needs. He'll sleep with the one he wants when he wants and if he is paying more attention to one than the other please speak up, but he will try to keep it even and honest. He had allowed the wives to control events up to now because he was at a loss on how to deal with the situation. It was simple now, both were his wives in equal status in his eyes. The girls agreed to his conditions and he took Lavon to bed the night after the honeymoon week was complete.

* * * * * * * * * *

Journal Entry, July 8th

I sit here at my desk at home and wonder what I did in this or another life to present me with two loving women. Alright, in the past it was illegal for a man to have two wives and I am sure someone is going to protest my situation especially in the job I have now.

Something I have never written about in my journal is how I have moved from being a simple carpenter to a position of such power as the Chief Marshall for New Mexico. I can only attribute how I deal with people to my parents and how they raised me. Keep it honest and fair to all people. I also think it was having Amanda around early on that cemented that into me. I did want her after a fashion and now looking back I was wanting Gwen back in my arms.

But the internal fight I had with right and wrong as far as Amanda was concerned drove me to act in a manner which drew the attention of others and brought me to the job I have now. Amanda called it right years ago when she said I was trying not to be a hypocrite in my actions and that built upon itself in everything else I did.

Now I have to thank both Lavon and Amanda for my waiting so long before Amanda and I took the final step. I no longer feel any guilt in my love for Amanda and even with the years between us in age, the passion of our love certainly shows itself at night, or any other time Amanda feels the need for me to make love to her.

Even Lavon's love making seems more aggressive and pleasurable for both of us now that the honeymoon is over between Amanda and myself. Lavon said she thought that she would be jealous of Amanda at first but was surprised when she wasn't.

I am wealthy in several ways now which surprises me. I only wanted to ensure that we had the things needed to survive and it has made me rich. I only sought to protect Amanda from the type of people that raped her mother and sister then took them away like cattle. Lavon entered our lives and she made my life easier while providing me with much pleasure.

If people dislike my having two wives, I'll give up everything to keep them. All I have done, all I have been doing since arriving in Santa Fe was to protect them from the evils of a world turned upside down.

* * * * * * * * *

Kevin made Amanda promise him one thing and that was regardless of how their life went she was not to even consider becoming pregnant until after her medical boards. Also, if she needed the time to study, he might sleep with her as long as it did not interfere with her studies. She agreed on both points then took him to bed.

The New Mexico Marshall's Service slowly developed into a strong law enforcement agency with a reputation for honesty and integrity. When it was brought up that Kevin had two wives, the wives themselves stood up and told the distractors to just shut up and stay out of his private life because as his wives they had no complaints.

Kevin now had two wedding anniversaries and did everything he could to be home for them as he also tried to be home for his son's birthdays. He bought an entire city block in a residential area of Albuquerque that had been devastated during the fighting and had the lots leveled and a new home build that could easily house the entire family to include a maid to help keep the house neat and clean. The grounds were maintained by a Mexican family with guidance from both Lavon and Amanda concerning flowers and other plants.

Just after his first anniversary of his marriage to Amanda, Kevin was sent to Nashville, where the new United States Capital had been set up for a conference with other states that were looking to set up Marshall Services such as New Mexico and a couple of other states had organized. Kevin spent a month in Nashville working on the charters of the other states patterning them after the one he had edited for New Mexico.

While he was gone, Lavon and Amanda slept with each other nightly even if they did not make love to each other. They had yet to show the kind of affection between each other in front of Kevin, but knew that one day they would have to treat him to a threesome just for fun.

April 12th

Ten Years After the End of the World

History shows that during the first months of the 'Event', American Naval forces around the world leveled whole cities in the countries that proclaimed credit for the attack on the United States with nuclear weapons. North Korea was finally rid of the dictatorship that had kept the country in ruin with South Korean forces immediately following up the American attacks on the country. The Middle East was a wasteland as Israel immediately took measures to prevent their own destruction with the American Mediterranean fleet finishing the job as ground fighting along the Israeli borders intensified.

Fighting broke out all through Europe as Muslims who had fled to those countries as refugees took up arms to destroy the countries they were in to bring them down and to be rebuilt as an Islamic state. As one country removed the internal threat, they moved to assist the countries still involved in removing the threat until nearly four years after the event, Europe was once again peaceful. Much of the historical artifacts of Europe was destroyed by the Islamic extremists in their attempts to remove all traces of history and replace them with their own warped take on history.

An attempt by a segment of the Mexican government sent troops into Texas, Southern New Mexico, Arizona, and California, in an attempt to reclaim lands they felt belonged to them, only to find the individuals living in those regions were determined not to give an acre to them. California suffered the worse but was finally ceded back to the United States after two years of guerilla warfare on both sides of the battle.

On Amanda's twenty-third birthday a celebration was held because the results of her medical boards had been reported and she had passed, earning her title as a Medical Doctor. She also informed Kevin that she was pregnant because once she had taken her boards, she saw no reason not to bring another child into the family. Carl and Walter were both in school when the wives took Kevin to bed for the afternoon, finally exposing the fact they had long been lovers when he was away.

* * * * * * * * *

Journey Entry, June 23rd.

Well today has certainly been eventful. Amanda received noticed she passed her Medical Boards and can practice medicine as a Doctor. There are not enough words to say how proud of her I am.

Next Amanda tells me she is pregnant, about a month along at this time. This was her choice, but I am very happy and hope everything goes good with this.

Now for the real shock of the day. The boys were at school and it seems the girls wanted me for lunch. Both at the same time. Now I have always had a suspicion that something was going on between them but today there is no doubt. It seems they have been lovers since before I married Amanda but have only slept together when I was gone being a Marshall. I'm exhausted but I guess I did my share because both wives left the bed happy with me.

I told Lavon and Amanda that they did not have to hide their relationship from me any longer, and they told me that we needed to get a larger bed, so they could sleep with me nightly, even if I only made love to one of them on any given night.

Karma has turned a bright light on me and now I wonder when the other shoe will drop. But it doesn't matter as I am going to enjoy my wives as long as possible.

* * * * * * * * *

Kevin's personal fortune had nearly tripled in the years of growth of the country as he expanded his business ventures outside the state into other states. He retired from public service the day Amanda gave birth to a blond headed girl which she named Allister after her own mother. The house in Santa Fe was razed with a new home build much like the one in Albuquerque. The house in Albuquerque was then turned into a library and art museum filled with the books and art works that Kevin had salvaged those first years.

Amanda became the Chief resident at an even newer hospital in Santa Fe and just before her thirtieth birthday gave birth to a son whom was named Jonathon. Kevin found out his uncle had survived the fighting around Denver and was settled back onto his farm there. His Uncle confessed that Kevin made the right choice in turning south as the danger at that time within the region was such he might have been killed by forces he would have joined since strangers were suspect.

Kevin returned to Kansas and the family farm making a claim on it based upon the documents he had buried and recovered. He had his parents remains dug up and properly buried then razed the remaining buildings to allow the ground to return to its natural state. He put the property in a family trust, so his children and grand-children would have a place if they desired as he also purchased the lands around it until he owned nearly a hundred square miles of land. He then leased the land to those who would farm it and produce the food for the people with five percent of the food going to a food bank so if anything like the Event took place again, there would be food available for the survivors.

Both he and Lavon received Honorable Discharges from their respective services at ranks two grades higher than when the event occurred. They both received numerous awards for that time even though Lavon stated all she had done was follow Kevin's lead.

There was a movement to draft Kevin in a run for the Governor's office, but he was explicit in that he had no desire to be in public service as he was having too much fun in retirement being around his children.

Amanda had one last child, a girl, when she was thirty-five. She was named Cynthia and Amanda had herself fixed to prevent any more pregnancies.

Kevin wrote his autobiography when he entered his sixties and never hid a thing as he told his own story from his viewpoint. He even expressed that on his wedding day to Amanda he felt a level of perversion in being with a girl her age even though so many girls her age had either already had children or were marrying. Kevin did hide many things concerning his relationship with Amanda prior to their wedding but he never hid his desire to be with her and gave his best memory of the first time he met her and saw her nude as she bathed.

His description of his early relationship with Lavon was pure carnal and over time that developed into a deep love for her. Kevin could never fully justify in his own heart and mind having two women such as he had in his life, but he accepted their love as he gave them all his heart. Even though the marriage to Amanda was Lavon's idea and completely accepted by Lavon, he said he always felt a touch of guilt when with Amanda although that passed in time. He never mentioned the relationship his wives had, and they never let that secret out of the bedroom. Any affection the wives showed towards each other in public was a sisterly hug and kiss on the cheeks.

When he addressed the comments of him being a profiteer during the recovery, his only comments were that his initial thoughts were to insure his family had what it needed to survive then slowly expanded that to the community. He put people to work when there wasn't any work and insured they had what they needed to do that job and provide for their families when others

196

were struggling from day to day. Kevin accepted no guilt for the families he could not help or the ones who felt others should take care of them.

Kevin's children grew tall and strong with the knowledge that family came before all others and each had to be able to take care of the others in a time of need. Knowledge was the key to survival and the simplest concepts were usually the best to provide what was needed to survive.

Kevin Barnes was a simple man with simple ideas for staying alive during a disastrous time for the world. Even as the world righted itself and he found himself with more wealth than he ever imagined, he never forgot who he was and where he came from.   The people of Santa Fe helped him keep his secret of wealth and anyone meeting him for the first time on the street only saw an elderly gentleman with polite manners.

Even his enemies from his early years treated him with respect as he had treated them when having to deal with them. No one ever seemed to notice there was always one younger man nearby who was ready to deal with anyone wanting to hurt him. This was his wives doing and he gave into them this as he had many other things over the years. But even if he seemed to be a gentle grandfather type he was always armed and still proficient with the old Sig pistol he carried from Kansas.

* * * * * * * * * *

Journal Entry, April 12th

Today is the 40th anniversary of the event which changed the world. In looking back at my early self, I wasted so much time mourning a love lost that I have finally recognized was nothing more than puppy love, if it could be called that. The event created a situation where the two greatest loves a man could have both entered my life and forever changed me. It was that drive to protect them, to insure their well-being that eventually brought me riches I never imagined.

I have two wonderful women to share my bed and comfort me. Four children that have grown strong and have chosen paths that can only make a parent proud. From them I have thirteen grand-children and out of them so far, I have five great-grand-children to spoil.

Thanks to both of my wives, I am still in good health as they worked hard to ensure that I could take care of them both in and out of bed.

I've given up trying to determine what I did to deserve my success or the love of Lavon and Amanda. No man knows where the path he walks will take him and my path still has years to travel but I will not have to travel it alone.

About the Author

Leon Michaels is the author of several novels and short stories that reflect his twenty-three years of military service. Michaels enlisted in the Marine Corps in 1970 and has memberships in the Veterans of Foreign Wars, the American Legion, the Disabled American Veterans organizations, NRA, and Rotary International. In 1971, he married his high school sweetheart, raised three daughters and has three grandsons. He calls Creek County, Oklahoma home.

Made in the USA
Columbia, SC
27 November 2017